THE THRE

"We Investigate Anything"

*

Jupiter Jones, Founder

*

Pete Crenshaw, Associate

*

Bob Andrews, Associate

The Three Investigators
Crimebusters
available in Armada

THE THREE INVESTIGATORS™

7

Reel Trouble

G. H. Stone
based on characters created by Robert Arthur

Armada

First published in the U.S.A. in 1989
by Random House, Inc.
First published in Great Britain in 1991 in Armada

Armada is an imprint of the Children's Division of
HarperCollins Publishers Ltd, 8 Grafton Street,
London W1X 3LA

Printed and bound in Great Britain by William Collins Sons
& Co. Ltd, Glasgow

1

Sour Notes

BOB ANDREWS WOVE THROUGH THE BUSTLING afternoon shoppers at the Rocky Beach Swap Meet. School had just ended for the year and Bob was ready for action!

Hot rock music sizzled in the warm June air. The band—the Hula Whoops—played the kind of great music that made your feet want to move. No wonder the Whoops had won a spot as finalists in next Saturday's big Jimmy Cokker Rock 'n' Roll Contest. Today they were at the swap meet as a paying gig.

Bob switched the cardboard box he was carrying from his left side to his right and did a little dance step. He was headed for the stage to meet his boss, Sax Sendler. This was a very exciting time for them. Sax owned Rock-Plus, Inc., a talent and management agency. He represented the Hula Whoops, and Bob was his number-one assistant!

Bob passed dozens of stalls where everything from hammers to jewelry to toys was for sale. The smell of popcorn filled the air. Often a pretty girl caught Bob's eye and smiled at him. Bob smiled right back.

"It's the teeth," said a voice at Bob's elbow.

"Huh?" Bob turned.

"All that orthodonture," his friend Pete Crenshaw continued. He'd been trotting after Bob to catch up. He couldn't help but see the array of cute girls Bob always seemed to attract. "Face it, guy. You've got a killer smile."

In his Talking Heads T-shirt and white jeans, seventeen-year-old Bob could pass for Mr. Teenage California, although he didn't try to. He was nearly six feet tall, tanned, blond, and blue-eyed. But his most potent weapon was charm. It radiated from him like heat from an oven.

"Terrific smile for a toothpaste ad," Pete added. "You'll look good on billboards."

Pete, who had a Walkman clipped to his dusty jeans, wore a T-shirt with an L.A. Lakers emblem. He was six feet one and weighed 190. He was in such great shape that he'd run the quarter mile from the parking lot without even breathing hard. Pete was feeling as good as Bob. He'd survived his geometry final—barely—and summer could begin.

"Forget my teeth," said Bob, "or I'll tell Kelly you've been looking at other girls."

"Wouldn't believe you," Pete said, brushing his reddish-brown hair from his forehead. Kelly Madigan was Pete's steady, a cheerleader. According to the guys' mutual pal, Jupiter Jones, she had big Pete wrapped around her little finger. "If *you're* around," Pete told Bob, "she knows *I* don't have a chance!"

Bob laughed, and they fell into step together. Bob

was meeting Sax to pick up publicity fliers to advertise the Whoops' appearance at the big contest. He'd promised to introduce Pete to the Hula Whoops if Pete would give him a lift home.

"Hey, don't forget," said Pete. "After here, we've got to get to work on your VW. What's the prob with it?"

"Are you kidding?"

"Sorry." Pete grinned. Bob was a champ with girls but a chump with cars. Pete eyed the loaded cardboard box Bob carried. "You got your own swap meet in there?"

"Just a few prized possessions."

"You cleaned out your locker today?"

"School's over. Didn't anybody tell you?"

"Sure, I threw everything away." Pete studied the pile. "Looks like you should've too."

In the box were ragged notebooks, old pens, papers, erasers, a battered cap, and Bob's first-semester science project—"The Life Cycle of the Fruit Fly." On top lay his empty backpack.

"I don't throw good money away," Bob said. Suddenly he noticed a banner over a swap meet stall to their right. The hand-lettered sign said: BARGAIN MUSIC TAPES! $2 EACH! 3 FOR $5!

"Hey, look!" Bob exclaimed.

Pete groaned.

"Come on," Bob said. He strode eagerly to the display table. Hundreds of music cassettes were spread out in rainbow colors. Bob set his cardboard box at his feet and began sorting through the tapes.

"What about Sax?" Pete said. "Forget him, what about your car? And Jupe's waiting for us!"

"There's plenty of time. Jupe's busy messing around with some new machine he found in Uncle Titus's last load of junk. He won't miss us."

Jupiter's guardians, Uncle Titus and Aunt Mathilda Jones, owned The Jones Salvage Yard. There, when they were just thirteen, Jupe, Pete, and Bob had founded The Three Investigators. Now, four years later, they were still at it—Rocky Beach's most famous and still youngest private detective trio.

"Need help?"

Bob looked into a pair of black eyes. The face that went with them was Asian, the nose narrow and the chin square. The guy's fingers drummed on the table, but not in time to the Hula Whoops' infectious beat. The guy was on edge.

"No, thanks. I want to look for a minute," Bob said. "You've got a great selection."

"Buy three, five bucks," the stallkeeper said. He had a slight singsong accent. But the words were toneless, and his gaze shifted to study the passing crowd as if he were watching for somebody.

"Speed it up," Pete ordered. "I want to meet the Hula Whoops!"

Bob picked a tape—an oldie by the Bushwhackers—then a reggae cassette from a Caribbean band, and finally a rap tape by the Watts Wonderfuls.

"Dy-no-mite!" Bob handed a five-dollar bill to the stallkeeper.

The stallkeeper tucked it away.

"O-*kay!*" Pete said. "Feet move! Rock stars, here I come!"

Bob grabbed his cardboard box and ran to catch up.

"You know," Pete said as they trotted up to the stage, "the Hula Whoops are really good!"

"Like I told you," Bob said. "Sax thinks they can win the Jimmy Cokker contest. That's ten thousand dollars, a six-week promo tour, and a record contract. The contract's super important. Could be the break that makes them."

"When's all this happening?"

"In three days. Saturday night in L.A."

At last the guys reached the center of the swap meet, which was a little hill with a stage on top. Now Bob could see there had to be a thousand stalls. People were laughing, dancing, eating cotton candy, and making deals—all to the lively beat of the Hula Whoops.

Bob and Pete walked around to the back of the stage, looking for Sax. It was quieter back there, and easier to talk. Pete tucked his T-shirt into his jeans. No, outside would look more cool, he thought. He pulled it out again.

"My man!" said a voice. And Sax Sendler emerged from behind a pile of amplifier cases. He was in his forties, dressed in his usual torn football jersey, black pants, and black lace-up hightops. His hair, pulled back in a ponytail, showed a few strands of gray. Officially Bob was Sax's part-time gofer, adviser on teenage tastes, and sometime roadie. It was the best job Bob had ever had—and the most fun.

"What you got there?" Sax asked Bob, his craggy face alight with interest. Once a hippie, now an entrepreneur, he was curious about everything.

"School junk," Pete said.

"And some tapes I've been after," Bob said. "I found them here. A real great deal."

He handed the three cassettes to Sax. "Someday our Whoops'll be doing these," Sax mused. He held out the three tapes to admire them.

Suddenly Bob leaned forward. "Oh, no!" he cried.

"What?" Pete said.

"The Bushwhackers' name is spelled wrong!"

"It is?" The label said *B u s h w a c k e r s*. It looked okay to Pete.

"The second *h* is missing!" Bob moaned.

"Hey, don't record companies have people that check spelling?" Pete asked.

"Right," Sax said. "Legit record companies don't let misspellings hit the market."

They examined the three cassette covers closely. The colors seemed less brilliant than they should have been, and the type was fuzzy around the edges. The print on one cover was faded typewriter type. The other two covers looked like color Xeroxes of originals. The Bushwhackers cover looked as if someone with little talent had painted it, misspelled the name, and then made color copies.

"We'd better listen to the tapes," Pete said grimly, and unclipped the Walkman from his belt.

He put one tape in, turned it on, and passed the earphones around. There was a low droning in the background that made their teeth ache. He put the second tape in. It sounded as if it was being played at too slow a speed and resembled moaning more than music. On the third tape the words were garbled nonsense.

Bob let out an anguished yell. "I've been ripped off!"

2

Rock 'Em, Sock 'Em

"**P**IRATES!" BOB EXCLAIMED.

"Could be, kid," Sax confirmed. "Some swap meets are heavy with knock-offs."

"Run that by me again?" Pete said, looking bewildered.

"Tape pirates," Bob answered. "They make copies from records or tapes and then sell the copies as originals. The quality usually stinks. Really ticks me off!"

"So what're you gonna do about it?" Sax asked.

Bob looked at Sax, then at Pete. He raised his chin. "I'm getting my money back!"

"Hey," Pete complained. "You were gonna introduce me to the Hula Whoops!"

"We'll be back by the time they wind up this set. Come on!"

Carrying his cardboard box, Bob strode down the swap meet aisle, muttering under his breath. Pete and Sax followed.

"Let's see this sleazeball," Sax said cheerfully. He loved a challenge.

"There's the tape stall," Bob said.

"Look!" Pete said. "Now there's two guys!"

The second guy was also Asian, but taller and stockier. He had a similar square jaw, a hard face, and a pale scar that swept from his left eye to his jawbone. It gave his face a mean, ugly expression. Or maybe, Bob thought as they approached, he really was mean and ugly.

The two pirates were hurriedly packing up and loading the open back of a blue Dodge van parked behind the stall.

Bob, Pete, and Sax stopped in front of the big display table. Most of the tapes were already packed. Bob looked around. None of the other stallkeepers were getting ready to leave.

"I'm returning these tapes," Bob said politely. "I'd like my money back. The tapes are obviously fakes." He held out the three cassettes. "That was five dollars."

The two men were working so fast they hardly glanced at the trio. The smaller one slipped cassettes into a box, his hands a blur of efficiency. The one with the scar loaded the box into the van, grabbed an empty one, and ran back to the table to pack more tapes. They were talking low in a language Bob didn't recognize. Their gazes constantly surveyed the crowd.

"Look, guys," Bob tried again, his voice louder, his grip on the cardboard box tighter. "These tapes stink. I want my five bucks back. Now!"

Again there was no response. For them, Bob didn't exist.

"Let's be reasonable," Sax said in his best reasonable-businessman voice. "These tapes are pirated. The kid wants his dough. You don't want trouble from the cops. So pay up. Make it easy on yourselves."

The larger guy, the one with the pale scar, raised his head. His hands paused. He spat out something harsh in the foreign language. He glared menacingly into Bob's eyes and snatched the three tapes from his hand.

"Hey!" Bob said, balancing his cardboard box as he tried to dive after the tapes.

But he was too late. The guy slammed Bob's tapes into the box he was packing and quickly shoved in more.

Pete bristled with indignation. He'd seen enough. The muscles in his neck corded as he worked to control his anger. He grabbed an arm of each pirate in midair and held them there.

"My . . . friend . . . wants . . . his . . . money," Pete said through clenched teeth. "Now."

Something happened to the two guys' faces. They seemed to collapse. Fear made them turn a sick shade of green.

It surprised Pete. And he relaxed his grip for a moment.

A moment was all they needed. They twisted free, scooped up the last of the tapes, and dumped them into the boxes. They ran toward the van.

Pete vaulted over the display table and went after them. Bob and Sax ran around the table after them, too.

And then they heard a shout. Pounding feet approached from behind.

Desperately the two pirates tossed their boxes into the van's open back. Glancing worriedly over his shoulder, the scar-faced one ran for the driver's seat. The smaller pirate slammed the rear doors closed.

Just as Pete reached the van, two new guys leaped over the display table after the pirates.

The first was a blond man with big feet, bushy eyebrows, and a bold, cool face. He knocked Sax and then Pete aside.

The second was another Asian, like the two pirates. He had a narrow, determined face, with fury glinting in his dark eyes.

The blond guy pulled the small pirate away from the rear of the van and socked him squarely in the jaw. The pirate went down. His attacker raced toward the driver's seat. He jumped up, grabbed the scar-faced pirate around the neck, and yanked him out of the van. They crashed to the ground.

Meanwhile the pirate at the rear of the van staggered to his feet. The Asian attacker swung a fist at him and yelled a question in the language that Bob didn't recognize. The tape pirate didn't answer. He ducked and tried to run away.

Pete, Bob, and Sax looked at one another.

"What gives?" Sax asked.

"Dunno," Pete said.

"Weird," Bob agreed. "If Jupe were here, he'd say it was a case for The Three Investigators."

The only response was the grunts and thuds of the brawl under way.

It was the two pirate stallkeepers against the two intruders. Pete wanted to help, but who were the good guys?

"Sax . . ." Pete began.

"No way, José," Sax said, crossing his arms. "I don't have a clue."

Around them, a crowd was gathering. The battle was going badly for the tape pirates. Suddenly the big pirate with the scar made a mad dash to escape, looking back over his shoulder at the blond guy, who was hot on his heels.

Bob saw the hefty pirate coming and started to step aside. But he was too late. The pirate crashed into Bob and bounced off. The blond guy chased him back toward the van.

Bob fell. His cardboard box crashed to the ground and skittered away almost into the next stall. His head hit something hard. His mind reeled in swirls of colors. Pain streaked red and blue behind his eyes.

3

Dazed and Confused

"BOB! HEY, BOB!"

Hazily Bob lifted his head. He saw Pete and Sax kneeling next to him, and . . . off to the side . . . someone trying to steal his cardboard box of school stuff! It was the smaller pirate. And the pirate seemed to be . . . floating! He and the cardboard box were floating a foot off the ground!

This was getting too crazy. Bob tried to get up. But his arms and legs weighed ten tons. Each. He closed his eyes.

"Bob!" Pete leaned close and shouted again.

"Hey, man!" Sax said. "Are you okay?"

Bob was lying flat on the ground. His head was inches from a metal toolbox that belonged to the next stall, where power tools were for sale.

"Ohhhh," he groaned, trying to rise.

Pete pressed him down.

"Don't try it," Sax told him. "Wait till you feel okay."

"Are they still fighting?" Bob asked. He opened his eyes, felt the bump on his head. "Owww!" Of all the dumb things for him to do—bang his head!

"Take a look," Sax said.

Bob rotated his head. "I can see," he said with

relief. The streaking lights were gone. And nobody was floating anymore. He could clearly see the large crowd that had gathered to watch the fight. The grunts and thuds were still going on.

Suddenly the pirate with the scarred face pulled a big wrench out of the back of the van. He swung it into the blond guy's stomach.

The blond guy doubled over, grunting with pain. Instantly the pirate slammed his fist up into the guy's jaw and made for the driver's seat. The motor roared to life.

The other pirate saw his chance. He kicked the Asian attacker one last time and broke free. He raced toward the van's passenger door and pulled himself inside. Instantly the van lurched away, spewing a brown cloud of dust behind it.

The Asian attacker leaped for the back-door handle in a last desperate attempt. But he was too late. His hand slipped off. He fell back and dropped to his knees in the dirt.

The blond guy staggered to his feet. There was no way either he or his cohort was going to catch the van. Furious, he kicked a display table. The van zipped through an opening in the crowd and sped off.

The blond man grabbed the smaller guy by the shoulder and snarled in his ear. The smaller man cringed and shook his head. The blond one snarled again, shoved him aside, and disappeared into the crowd.

The smaller man watched, his face fearful. Then he melted into the throng in the opposite direction.

"I can kiss my five dollars good-bye," Bob said.

"Wow!" Pete said. "What was that all about?"

"Remember when I bought the tapes?" Bob said. "The guy who sold them to me kept watching the crowd for something—or someone."

"You think he knew the other two guys were at the swap meet?" Pete said.

"Maybe he was worried they were. Maybe that's why the second pirate came later—he was scouting for them."

Pete nodded slowly. "I'll buy that."

Bob started to get up, gingerly feeling the bump on the back of his head.

Sax and Pete helped him.

"Go slow, Rambo," Pete warned.

"I've only got time for one brawl today, anyway," Bob said. "I've got a date with Jana later."

Pete rolled his eyes but looked relieved that his friend was back in form.

"Don't forget your stuff," Pete said, walking off to retrieve the cardboard box and handing it to Bob.

"Right," Bob said.

Sax dusted off his black pants. He liked his pants to be *very* black.

The crowd had dwindled to a few diehards who stood around the empty display table. They were enthusiastically retelling the fight to one another. For them it was the high point of the swap meet.

"Hey, maybe the two guys hit on the pirates because they were ripped off like you were," Pete suggested.

"Sounds like a great idea to me," Bob said. "Man, would I like to get *my* hands on those pirates!"

"Stay cool," said Sax. "First we got work to do."

"The Whoops!" said Pete.

Bob, Pete, and Sax headed back toward the stage where the Hula Whoops jumped, gyrated, and played their dazzling rock 'n' roll. Everything seemed noisily normal. The swap meet was so large that only a fraction of the people there had been aware of the fight.

"Maybe Blondie and his sidekick were angry musicians," Sax went on. "You know, we got copyright laws against stealing other dudes' work—not just songs, but books, movies, all that stuff. Like, the Whoops write their own numbers. They deserve to make a buck if somebody records their songs."

"Wouldn't it be great if somebody did record them!" said Bob. "Or if they got their own recording contract. They're not exactly rolling in money."

"Don't I know it!" said Sax. "And I sure would be mad if somebody pirated them."

"Is there that much pirating going on?" asked Pete.

" 'Fraid so," said Sax. "We got a real problem around here. A little while ago a guy in L.A. was convicted of selling tape knock-offs. The paper said his operation was so big it cost the record industry about thirty-two *million* bucks in lost sales of legit tapes."

Pete whistled. "That's a lot of tamales."

"And that doesn't count what the artists—the composers, the singers, the musicians—lost in royalties," added Sax. When you turn copying into a business and sell your knock-offs, you're really hurting people."

Bob and Pete nodded.

They were nearing the stage. People were packed

together, some dancing, others listening. The pulsating rock sounds were irresistible. Above them, the Hula Whoops were just finishing a song. Bob slid his cardboard box under the rear stage floorboards for safekeeping.

"It's hard to do business when the Whoops are around," Sax announced. "Soon as they start the next set I'll get out the fliers. You haven't met the Whoops yet, Pete?"

"Not yet." Pete hoped he didn't look as awkward as he felt. He could hold his own with a football team. Performers were something else.

"Bet they rattle your chains," Sax said. He grinned in anticipation.

The music came to a clean, crisp end. A perfect final beat. The audience broke into loud applause and whistles. The Whoops bowed low, unhooked their instruments, and ran off the stage.

The applause grew thunderous. They ran back on, bowed four more times, and waving broadly, exited down the stairs behind the stage.

"Hey! Hey! Hey!" shouted a tall, thin young man with long cornsilk hair and a flowing beard. He pounded Sax on the back with one hand. In the other he shook a pair of drumsticks. "How'd we do, man? I mean, really, weren't we hot?"

"You're always hot, Tony," Sax said as he good-naturedly absorbed the pounding. "Red hot. This is Tony," he told Pete. "Drummer. The dude with the magical sticks. Everybody, this is Bob's friend Pete Crenshaw."

Pete nodded shyly.

Tony tapped a complicated rhythm on the edge of the stage with his sticks. His white shirttails flapped over his tattered jeans.

"Hear it?" he said. "Don't you love it? Seventeen-eight time!"

"Cosmic, man," Sax said with respect. "And here's Maxi," he told Pete. He smiled down at a tiny young woman, barely five feet tall.

"Vocals," Maxi sang. She had a very pretty heart-shaped face, long black hair, and a tight red-leather dress with padded shoulders and no sleeves. It looked as if she'd torn the sleeves out, Pete decided. She had nice arms beneath the ragged leather openings, and she wrapped them around Sax's middle. She squeezed.

"Great vocals," Sax squeaked.

"Only great?" She pouted. She squeezed harder.

"The *greatest*."

Maxi grinned and released him.

"And I mean it," Sax went on. "Three-octave range. This little lady belts a mean song."

Maxi smiled sweetly. She reached up and patted Bob's cheek. Bob smiled—a lot.

No wonder he likes this job, Pete thought. He's getting paid to let pretty girls be nice to him!

Pete hadn't been the only one to watch Bob and Maxi.

"Romance is a thing of the past," announced a guy with a shaved head. "The nuclear age has time only for momentary interfaces."

"This is Quill," Sax said. "Keyboardist. Everything

from organ music to raindrops. The guy's an orchestra in himself."

Quill bowed solemnly to Pete. Sunlight gleamed on his shiny shaved head and on a small gold hoop earring in his right ear. In fact, all the Whoops had a gold hoop in their right ear. Quill wore an old tuxedo with white clothesline rope for a belt. There were gaping holes in the knees of his trousers. To Pete he looked like a hip scarecrow.

"Life is essentially meaningless," Quill continued. "We've become mere protoplasm for the intergalactic synthesizer."

Pete didn't know what to say. This was like no conversation he'd ever had. But he couldn't wait to tell Kelly about it.

"Don't worry about Quill," Maxi told Pete. "Nobody understands him."

Maxi pulled forward a handsome guy in a stained tweed sports coat, tight white corduroy pants, and cowboy boots.

"Here's Marsh," she said to Pete.

He had disheveled brown hair, a high, intelligent forehead, and smoldering gray eyes.

"Guitarist and composer," Sax said proudly. "This is the dude who writes most of the Whoops' music. Need I say more?"

"I'm impressed," Pete said honestly. "And I sure hope you guys win Saturday night."

"Saturday night?" Marsh echoed. His brow suddenly creased. His smoldering eyes turned vacant. "What's Saturday night?"

"The Jimmy Cokker contest," Sax said, amused. He explained to Pete, "Marsh sometimes has a hard time relating to reality. He's too wrapped up inside his head. Writing music. Right, man?"

"Yeah, the absent-minded professor," Maxi chimed in.

"Can't," Marsh said. He looked embarrassed.

"Can't what?" Sax said.

"Can't play Saturday night," Marsh explained. "I'm getting married then. Yeah. We decided last night. Eight o'clock, I think. Guess we'll have to call off the gig."

4

The Dating Game

THEY WERE STUNNED.

"What!" Maxi screeched.

"This blows it!" Tony yelled.

What was Marsh thinking of? This contest would give the band its widest exposure ever. And if they won, the tour and record contract would launch the Whoops into the big time!

Sax and Bob tried to reason with Marsh. Tony questioned his sanity. Quill discussed the meaninglessness of marriage. Maxi pouted and tapped her foot. And through it all, Marsh refused to yield. It was *his* life and he wouldn't call off the wedding. End of discussion.

Suddenly Maxi erupted again. "Idiot!" she screamed. She pounded Marsh's chest. "Selfish jerk!" She slapped his face and stalked off.

Surprised at her fury, the guys stopped arguing. They watched her small haughty back hustle away.

"*I quit*," she flung over her shoulder. "Go find someone else to finish singing the gig *today*!"

That brought them up short. They needed Maxi, Pete realized, just as much as they needed Marsh. Now even Marsh was worried.

"Hold it, girl!" Sax said, chasing Maxi.

He grabbed her arm. She yanked free, stepped back, and crossed her arms over her red-leather dress. Waiting. Her angry eyes telling them all—this had better be good!

"You're a pro," Sax said sternly. "You've got another set."

"Big deal. So's Marsh. That didn't stop him from blowing our big chance Saturday night! Later!"

"Maxi!" Bob said. "Wait a minute!"

He trotted up to her, leaned over, and whispered in her ear. She shook her head furiously. Then she nodded once. Then twice more.

Sax returned to Marsh and poked him in the chest.

Marsh looked sheepishly at his agent. Maxi had definitely gotten to him. "Yeah?"

"What's your fiancée's name?" Sax asked.

"Carmen Valencia."

"Carmen Valencia!" Maxi yelled. "Her? You're going to marry *her*?"

"It's cool. I know Carmen," Sax said. "I'm phoning her and we're changing the date."

"She'll be mad," Marsh warned, but he looked relieved. "She's got a serious temper."

"Temper!" Maxi bellowed indignantly. "That ain't the half of it, bud. That songbird couldn't carry a tune in a *bucket*!"

Pete suppressed a grin.

Sax checked his watch. "Time, guys." He was all business. "Next set. Let's go."

Marsh, the creator of all the turmoil, sighed, exhausted. He brushed some hair off his handsome face. "What're we playing this set?"

As they trooped back up to the stage, Tony listed the songs.

Quill settled behind the keyboards. *"Pax vobiscum,"* he said in Latin. "Peace be with you." And he smiled beatifically at Sax.

"There's a lot more action here than in a Lakers game," Pete said.

"They're usually not this wild," Bob admitted.

"Yeah," Sax agreed. "The wedding's a mind-blower. But we'll get it straightened out."

"Marsh sounded so . . . laid-back about it," Pete said. "I mean, he made it seem like going out for a pizza."

Sax shrugged. "That's Marsh. He's been engaged maybe a dozen times. This one'll probably never happen either."

"What'd you say to Maxi?" Pete asked Bob. "How'd you get her mellowed out?"

"Easy," Bob said. "Marsh's been engaged twice to Maxi. And she broke it off both times. But just because she's not marrying him doesn't mean she'll let him marry someone else. So I told her he probably got engaged because he's nervous about the big gig. That he probably still loves only her. And she should be patient until he figures it out himself."

"Ever think of filling in for Dear Abby?" Pete kidded.

"Blow it out your ear," Bob retorted.

Then a chord sounded from Marsh's guitar. In an instant music burst clean and pure from the four mu-

sicians. Another great song from the Hula Whoops.
Pete wondered whether you had to be wacko to be a
dynamite rock musician. Then he decided it didn't
matter. The Whoops' music was the hottest!

"Come on," Sax said, and started talking like an
agent. "Okay. Here's the strategy for Saturday night. I
want hundreds of Rocky Beach fans to show up for the
Whoops at the L.A. Forum." He handed Bob a stack
of bright yellow fliers. "When judges hear crowds
raving for a band, they're impressed. So stick these up
all over town. Like now."

"How about first thing in the morning?" Bob asked.
"My car's dead."

"I'm gonna fix it today," Pete vowed.

"Okay," Sax said, "you're on. But first thing tomorrow!" He turned to look at the stage where the Whoops
played and danced in perfect rhythm with the
music—and with one another. "Those kids are sometimes off the wall, but they're dynamite musicians.
They can take that contest!"

◆   ◆   ◆

Pieces of an old reel-to-reel tape machine were spread
on the table in front of Jupiter Jones. The breadbox-
size gizmo was an ancestor of modern cassette players.
Its innards were arranged in the sequence in which
Jupe had disassembled them. There was nothing really
wrong with the machine, he'd decided, except that it
was old and needed cleaning and adjusting. And when
he'd finished, he'd have a great piece of equipment.
One that would produce studio-quality sound, the
kind records could be made from.

"But what're you gonna *do* with it?" Pete asked.

Jupe airily waved the question aside while Bob watched, amused. "Something will occur to me," Jupe said with his usual confidence. "Perhaps Uncle Titus and I will simply sell it for a nice profit."

The three guys were at The Jones Salvage Yard. Jupe was working in his electronics workshop, a shack that stood just outside the trailer that served as their headquarters. A dish antenna topped the roof, and high-tech electronic devices and parts lined shelves and countertops.

At the other end of the trailer was the informal grease pit where Pete and Jupe's second cousin Ty Cassey—when he was in town—worked on cars for themselves, friends, and, occasionally, paying customers. Jupiter and Bob strolled over to watch Pete work on Bob's VW.

"Rats. I'm bombing out on this one," Pete said. He stood up, hands on his waist, and peered down at the rear-end engine of Bob's ancient red Volkswagen Beetle. The car wouldn't start yesterday afternoon. Fortunately Bob had been parked right in front of the salvage yard. He and Jupe had pushed it inside to await Pete's help.

"Do my ears deceive me?" Bob cried. "Does supermechanic Pete Crenshaw admit defeat?"

"Lay off," Pete said. "Ty'll know how to fix it. When's he coming back, Jupe?"

"No one's heard from him," Jupe said. "That's usually a sign that he's on his way home."

Ty Cassey was twenty-seven and a crack mechanic.

But he also had itchy feet. Now that he made the junkyard his home base, the guys knew they could count on him showing up for a week or so once a month. He'd been gone three weeks. So they expected him any day.

"Is my car history?" Bob said. "I mean, it's not just because I'm supposed to put up those fliers tomorrow. I want to go back to the swap meet today, see if I can track down those crummy tape pirates. I'm still steamed about my five bucks. And tonight Jana and I were going to the movies . . ."

"Better find out if she's got a car," Pete said.

"Brother." Bob headed into the trailer and Jupiter went back to his workshop.

"The choke valve's working," Pete muttered into the engine. "The automatic choke's working. The throttle valve's working. So what's wrong?"

"Jupe," Bob called from the trailer doorway, phone in hand, "Jana says she'll drive, but she's got a girl-friend who wants to go too. How about it?"

"What do you mean, 'How about it?' " Jupe replied. "Jana's friend doesn't need my permission to go to the movies."

"Don't be dense," Bob said.

Jupiter knew exactly what Bob meant. But he would rather be held at knifepoint in a dark alley than go on another excruciating blind date.

Pete couldn't resist hearing how Jupe would weasel out of this one. He went over to the workshop.

"I'm too busy," Jupe announced, lowering his nose toward the reel-to-reel machine.

"Jupe says he's too busy," Bob said into the phone. "What? Okay, sure." Bob turned to Jupe. "She wants to talk to you. Come on, Jupe. Hang loose."

Jupiter mumbled under his breath about hanging Bob instead. Slowly he laid down his screwdriver. He pushed himself back from the table. He stood. He had black hair, a round face, and . . . well . . . as he liked to put it, a robust girth. His great intelligence seemed able to conquer everything but his hefty weight—and his shyness with girls.

He reached for the workshop telephone extension and cleared his throat. "Jupiter Jones speaking." His solemn face was turning pink. "Nice to make your acquaintance." He closed his eyes and swallowed. "No, I'm not a Scorpio. . . . This evening, unfortunately, I have other plans that cannot be changed."

"Jupe!" Pete and Bob yelled at the whopper.

Jupiter ignored them. "Thank you very much for thinking of me." He hung up his extension and wiped the sweat off his forehead.

Bob rolled his eyes at Jupe and said into his phone, "Seven o'clock, sure. Can't wait to see you either! Bye, Jana!" Bob hung up and rejoined his friends.

"I've already seen the movie," Jupe announced, "and the book was much better." He picked up his screwdriver and went back to work. "Besides, I have a new eating program." He'd decided that "diet" was too negative a word. "It's called the Bread and Butter Eating Program, because I get to have a slice of bread and butter with every meal. If I go to the movies, I'll end up eating popcorn, peanuts, and candy bars, too.

I don't want to blow two whole weeks of self-restraint."
He tugged at his waistband hopefully, but it was as
snug as ever.

Bob and Pete looked at each other, grinned, and
shrugged with resignation. Once Jupe made up his
mind, it was like trying to budge Mount Whitney to
make him change it.

"And another thing," Jupe continued. "I want to
think more about what happened today. Why did you
shell out good money for those pirated tapes anyway,
Bob?"

"They were three for five dollars," Bob said. "It was
a steal."

"You can say that again," Pete retorted, and they all
laughed.

"You wanted something for nothing," Jupe sniffed.
"But nothing is what you got."

"Give me a break, Jupe. You like bargains too. It
isn't fair to con people that way. I work hard for my
bread."

"Were the two guys who attacked the stallkeepers
customers too?" Jupe asked.

"What else could they be?" Pete asked.

"Don't know," Jupe said. "But angry customers
usually want their money back. Did they ask for it?"

"One of them yelled something," Bob said, "but it
was in a foreign language."

"Zero help," Jupe pronounced. "Did either of you
get the license plate number of the Dodge van?"

Pete gulped. Bob stared sheepishly at Jupe.

"No," they both admitted.

Jupiter shook his head sadly at such rank amateurism. "Perhaps there's a clue you missed. A word. An action. Or something you simply forgot."

"I didn't call Kelly!" Pete yelped, running into Headquarters for privacy. "She'll think I *forgot her!*"

"You *did* forget her," Jupe called after him with maddening logic. He cleaned a screw thoughtfully and pondered the events of the swap meet. He had a feeling that the fight was important. There was more at stake here than getting Bob's money back. This was becoming a case for The Three Investigators.

Bob was thinking about it too. About ripoff tape pirates. About how dumb and gullible he'd been. All of which made him totally disgusted. And furious. Suddenly he had a vague memory of seeing something weird after he'd been knocked down. Something floating. What was it?

And then he hit upon an idea so simple and perfect that he smacked his forehead.

"Hey!" Jupe said, surprised. "What gives?"

Bob grabbed the workshop extension, ordered Pete to get off the line, and asked for the number of the swap meet business office. He found a pen in his pocket but no paper, so he wrote the number on his hand.

He quickly dialed the phone. "The sixth aisle from the stage," he said, his face animated. "Yes, that's it! A cassette-tape stand!" He wrote some more information on his hand. "Thanks a lot!" He hung up.

Excited, Bob said, "The stall was registered to a Prem Manurasada. And he lives at 434 San Martin Drive, Rocky Beach!"

Jupe picked up the phone book, turned pages, and ran his finger down a column of names. "There's no Prem Manurasada in the directory." He called Information, but they didn't have a listing either.

"What about the address?" Bob wasn't ready to give up. Not yet!

"Let's check the computer," Jupe said. "I have a cross-referenced city directory on disk."

Bob and Jupe walked into Headquarters. Jupe kept his computer there because the trailer was air-conditioned.

"But Kelly," Pete was pleading on the phone, "I *do* remember you. All the time."

The other two Investigators exchanged glances, and Jupe turned on the computer. His fingers flew on the keyboard. Information appeared and disappeared on the screen.

Finally Jupe said, "Here's the answer—but you're not going to like it. There's a 432 and a 436 San Martin Drive. But there's *no* 434!"

"What does that mean?" Bob said.

"It's either a vacant lot, or the street's so crowded they didn't have room for a 434."

Bob groaned. "Our only lead! And it's phony!"

Jupe nodded, his eyes gleaming.

"That won't stop me," Bob said decisively. "I'm going to nail those ripoff artists—no matter what!"

5

A Reel Mystery

THE NEXT MORNING BOB AWOKE WITH A START. Warm sunlight streamed through his window and across his bed. He was supposed to put up the Hula Whoops' fliers first thing this morning. And he'd completely forgotten! He'd had a great time at the movies with Jana last night and had forgotten everything else. What a jerk!

He looked at his digital clock: 10:00. Boy, was he late! And he still didn't have a car!

Thinking hard, he threw on his clothes and . . . he had it. The solution!

The Andrews house was quiet as he ran into the upstairs hall. His dad and mom had both gone to work. His dad was a reporter, and his mom was a realtor.

He picked up the phone and dialed.

"Hi, Sax," he said, and cleared his throat. "Remember my car was broken down?" he said. "Well, Pete couldn't fix it . . . and I was wondering whether . . . I could borrow . . . the hearse." He held his breath.

"Sure, kid," Sax said. His voice sounded harried. "It's the company car. But get your carcass over here quick. We gotta talk." And Sax hung up.

Bob heaved a sigh of relief. Sax was a great boss. Bob hurriedly grabbed the fliers. He'd ride his bike to Sax's. He could carry the fliers in his backpack.

He pulled out the cardboard box filled with his school stuff from under the bed. The empty backpack was on top. He was starting to put the fliers inside it when he saw a strange thing.

A brown paper sack was wedged among the stuff under the backpack. The sack wasn't his. He opened it. Inside were two narrow white boxes labeled AMPEX, 1/4-INCH TAPE. He opened one box and found a reel of tape about ten inches across.

Quickly he looked inside the other box. It held an identical reel. On the plastic centers someone had written REEL 1, REEL 2 with a white grease pencil.

He stood for a moment and stared. How did they get into the box of his school stuff? And what were they?

Then Sax's voice echoed in his mind: "Get your carcass over here quick."

He slid the fliers into his backpack. Soon he was speeding away on his bicycle, the paper sack with the reels under his arm.

He pedaled into The Jones Salvage Yard, ran to Jupe's workshop, opened the sack, and spilled the white boxes onto the table in front of Jupe.

"What . . . " Jupe began, a piece of bread and butter suspended in his hand.

"Hey, Jupe, give these the once-over, okay? I gotta move. They turned up in the box of stuff I was carrying at the swap meet yesterday. Might be important. I don't have time to . . . "

Jupiter's eyes shone. "Say no more." He popped the bread into his mouth, picked up one of the boxes, and turned it from side to side intently. It was just the kind of challenge Jupiter thrived on. He opened the box.

Bob hopped back on his bike and pedaled furiously to Sax's house, which was only a mile away. Half the house served as the office for Rock-Plus, Inc.

Trees, pedestrians, and parked cars passed in a blur.

And then, a block from Sax's, a big blue Dodge van came up alongside Bob. It took a few seconds for the van to register in Bob's distracted mind.

And then he remembered.

The van was just like the one the tape pirates had escaped in the day before!

An Asian face peered out of the passenger side. It was the guy who'd sold Bob the three tapes! What was he doing here?

"Hey!" Bob yelled. "You turkey! Give me my five bucks back!"

The man looked startled and ducked his head back into the van. "Prem!" he squealed to the person in the driver's seat. It was the scar-faced pirate. Bob heard fragments of a hurried conversation in the unfamiliar foreign language. This time he wasn't going to be a jerk. He tried frantically to get a look at the license plate. Drat! The van was right next to him, so all he could see was the side panel.

Suddenly the van put on a burst of speed. The rear came into view. Below the back doors Bob could make out . . . nothing. Mud covered the license plate. The van raced around a corner and disappeared.

Cursing to himself, Bob pedaled on to Sax's house. What the heck was going on?

◆   ◆   ◆

Bob and Celeste Fayley sat in canvas chairs in Sax's office. Autographed photos of his artists and groups filled the walls. Behind his desk, Sax paced like a caged animal between the old upright piano in one corner and the elaborate stereo outfit in the other. The agent ran his fingers through his hair, and his usually warm face settled into a worried frown.

"So that's the story, kids," he told them. "I gotta fly to Omaha to see my mom for a few days. The surgery's no big deal, but somebody needs to be there and make sure she's taken care of." He stopped and leaned toward them over his desk. He tried to smile. "You two're gonna have to run the office. I know you'll do a dynamite job."

"What about the Hula Whoops?" Bob asked.

"I'll be back Saturday morning. Just keep 'em from killing each other or marrying someone else, okay?"

"Okay." Bob grinned.

"I filled in Celeste about yesterday," Sax said.

"Maxi and Marsh are really hysterical," Celeste said. She was tall, blond, statuesque, and gorgeous. She was also a college student, and Sax's part-time secretary. "Think they'll ever get together?"

"I don't know if the world's ready for the combination," Sax said. "Could be volcanic."

They laughed. Then the office doorbell tinkled.

"Were you expecting anyone?" Celeste asked Sax on her way to the door.

"No. And I'm outta here." Sax fished a dusty tooled-leather briefcase from beneath his desk. He shoved papers into it. "Have to leave enough room for my underwear," he muttered to himself.

Bob stood up.

"Oh, yeah. The hearse." Sax tossed keys across the desk. "When you're done, give the keys to Celeste. And don't worry too much about the Whoops. I'm counting on you to do any hand-holding that's needed, but they should be fine. About one blow-up a week is their max."

"Boy, I hope so," Bob said fervently.

Sax walked around his desk. "So long."

Sax's door opened. "Mr. John Henry Butler to see you," Celeste said.

"Just for a mini-second, Sendler," twanged a nasal voice from the outer office, behind Celeste. "I know your time is precious. If I might just squeeze my tiny self into your too-too busy day. If you could spare me a moment to chat about this sensational young group you've got—the, uh, Hula Whoops."

Celeste stood square in the doorway. She wasn't going to let Butler past until she had Sax's okay.

Sax rolled his eyes and smacked his forehead. "What timing," he muttered.

John Henry Butler was one of the most powerful critics of the pop music scene in Southern California. His reviews and essays appeared twice weekly in the biggest Los Angeles newspaper. Everybody read him. He could make a group in L.A. with one sentence.

Sax made up his mind. "Jack!" he said, radiating

warmth as he brushed past Celeste. "How wonderful of you to drop by. Please come in. Celeste, coffee?"

Bob stood out of the way as Sax led a short, pudgy man back into his office.

"Mr. Butler, I'd like you to meet my associate, Bob Andrews."

"Charmed. Might I be meeting an actual Whoop?" Butler, in his early fifties, eagerly looked Bob up and down. He had tiny blue eyes, a fringe of gray hair above his ears, and a strong scent of expensive perfume.

"My assistant," Sax reminded Butler.

Bob put out his hand. "Actually, Sax is being kind. I'm his gofer."

"Oh!" Butler almost retracted his hand. But he allowed Bob to squeeze his fingers. Then he quickly put his hand into the pocket of his silk suit.

Probably to sanitize it, Bob thought, but said politely, "Nice to meet you, sir."

"I'm sure it was." Butler looked at Sax and smiled. "I'm toying with the idea of announcing the Hula Whoops as my super favorites to win the Cokker contest. Wouldn't you just *love* it?"

Sax's mouth fell open. Quickly he closed it. "An excellent choice, Jack. Very perceptive."

Butler examined both canvas chairs, then oozed his expensively clad bottom into one. Sax, his craggy face pink with excitement, went back behind his desk and sat down too. Bob slipped into the outer office, quietly closing the door behind him.

The walls of the outer office held booking charts

and more framed photographs of the groups Sax handled. But Bob noticed only Celeste. She was in a temper. She slammed two ceramic mugs onto her desk and angrily grabbed for the coffee pot on a filing cabinet.

Celeste's eyes flashed. "He pinched me! Can you believe it? When he was standing behind me at the door, that smelly old man pinched me! He is so gross. If he didn't mean so much to Sax's business, I'd have belted him one!"

"You're right," Bob said. "He *is* a creep." He squeezed her shoulder. "But at least he shows good taste in choosing you to pinch."

"Thanks a lot. He has no business pinching *any-one*!" She threw some sugar packets and spoons onto a tray. "Let that stinkball get his own coffee. He's disgusting, you know? He looks like a big fat white toad!"

Bob laughed. Butler *did* look like a fat, pasty toad. Celeste began to laugh too.

◆　　　◆　　　◆

Bob drove the polished black hearse down Main Street. Wherever he went, people stopped and stared at the long, elegant automobile. Built in 1969, it was a Cadillac with a Fleetwood body. Sax had bought it at an auction more than ten years ago, added a back seat, and restored it to impeccable condition. The soft leather upholstery was original, and the dashboard was gleaming black walnut. It was Sax's personal car, but sometimes he used it to transport acts, too.

Bob brought the hearse to a sedate stop at a parking

meter and got out with his backpack. This part of
Main Street was lined with fast-food joints where teenagers and college students hung out. It was a perfect
place to alert the Whoops' fans that the band was
performing in a big contest.

He walked up one side of the street and down the
other, getting permission to tape the fliers in store
windows, pin them on bulletin boards, and staple
them to message poles.

After an hour of this, Bob stopped in a donut shop.
He put up a flier, then stood in line to buy a butter-
milk donut fresh from the oven.

His backpack in one hand and one bite left of the
donut in the other, he entered an alley to cross over to
Grand Avenue. There he could put up the fliers in
bookstores and coffee shops. He finished the donut
and licked his fingers.

He'd taken about twenty steps down the bricked
alley when he heard a strange rustling in a dark re-
cessed doorway. He hesitated, then started to turn.

Suddenly a thick black cloth dropped over his head.

His backpack was snatched away, and steely hands
pinned his arms to his sides.

He couldn't see or move!

6

Fast Forward

STUNNED, BOB STOOD HELPLESS IN A SUFFOCATING black world of strange muffled sounds and no words. Whoever held him said nothing and seemed to do nothing.

"Who are you?" he said loudly, forcing his voice to remain calm. He heard rustling. Suddenly he realized his legs were free.

And he was being held from behind!

In a smooth, practiced motion, Bob leaned forward against the hands. He knifed back a karate *ushiro-kekomi* back-thrust kick.

His foot met flesh. He heard a terrible groan.

Reflexively the steel hands released him and he fell forward. Feet pounded away down the alley. He thanked his stars that he and Pete had been practicing their karate regularly.

He ripped off the black shroud. But the alley was empty. Had he heard one set of feet—or two?

He picked up his backpack and stared down at the pile of fliers on the ground. Whoever had attacked him had deliberately opened the backpack and dumped them out. Bob knew that because he'd zipped the backpack shut while waiting in line at the donut shop.

Why would anybody be so desperate to see the fliers? Or had they been looking for something else? Like the two reels of tape he'd found among his school things that morning!

◆ ◆ ◆

It was two thirty that afternoon when Bob pedaled his bike into the salvage yard. He'd dropped off the hearse and checked with Celeste that the Hula Whoops were calm. Now he was in a hurry to tell Jupe about the attack in the alley—and to ask about the tapes.

As he rode through the junkyard's gates he almost fell off his bike. Magnificent, clear rock 'n' roll was pouring out of the workshop.

He coasted over to Jupe and Pete. They were sitting inside the electronics shack, hands behind their heads, chairs tilted back, feet up on the worktable as they listened to the crystalline notes. A plate with a few telltale crumbs sat on the table.

"Is that the Barbarians?" Bob asked in a hushed voice.

"Shhhh!" Pete said.

Jupe didn't bother to answer. He didn't often like rock, but now he was lost in another world, his eyes closed. This was almost as good as bread and butter!

Bob leaned his bike against his VW and sat on a stool. The music was coming from the old reel-to-reel machine Jupe had been fixing the day before. Bob leaned over to get a look at the reel spinning off the sounds. Unless he was blind or crazy, it was one of the two he'd given Jupe that morning to I.D.!

"Guys . . . " he began.

"Shhhh!" Pete and Jupe said in unison.

Bob nodded and closed his eyes too. They were right. He could ask questions later. Now all he wanted was to be bathed in the remarkably high-quality sound of this great music.

There was a moment of awed silence after the reel finished playing.

"So that's what your reel-to-reel machine is for," Bob said to Jupe.

Jupiter smiled smugly. "Amazing, isn't it? All this piece of equipment really is, is an overgrown, higher-quality, faster-speed cassette player. Of course, there are some technical differences . . ."

"Later, Jupe," Pete said. If he let Jupe go on, they'd be in for a twenty-minute lecture. "We need some hard info first. Where'd you get the reels, Bob?"

Bob told them about finding the paper sack wedged among his school stuff in his cardboard box.

"Who could've put them there?" Pete wondered.

"That's what I want to know," Bob said. "Guess who I saw this morning." Bob described the blue Dodge van that drove alongside him on the way to Sax's, and the two pirates inside.

"The big guy with the scar must be Prem Manurasarda," finished Bob. "At least, the smaller pirate called him Prem."

"Did you—" Jupe began.

"I can read your mind, Jupe," Bob interrupted. "The van had mud all over its license plate, so there was no number to check."

"That's against state law," Jupe said.

"When you've already stolen tapes, robbed some-one's five bucks, and knocked somebody else's guts out with a wrench, what've you got to lose?" Pete retorted.

"I've got another weirdness to run by you guys," said Bob. He told them how he was attacked in the alley earlier that day.

Jupe pulled on his lower lip, a sign of deep thought. "An odd series of events, apparently unconnected."

"The fight at the swap meet has gotta have some-thing to do with it," Pete suggested.

"Wait a minute!" Bob said. He ran his fingers through his blond hair. He was starting to remember . . . he'd seen something floating after he fell and hit his head during the fight. He saw . . .

Jupe and Pete watched Bob intently.

"I—I remember the smaller pirate . . . floating off the ground . . . and squatting beside my cardboard box. Later I thought he was trying to steal it. But maybe he was stashing something in it instead!"

"Hmmm," Jupe said. His round face suddenly brightened. "Let's make a hypothesis," he announced, "that these reels are what tie the events together. Try this out. The four men at the swap meet were fighting about the reels. One pair had the reels, and the other pair wanted them. If you really saw a pirate beside your box, Bob, then we can assume the pirates had the reels first, and the two men who attacked were after them."

"Okay," Bob said. "But how come the pirates' van was driving beside me this morning?"

"They must've traced you!" Pete said. "Did you talk about Sax or the Hula Whoops while you were buying the tapes?"

"I could've," Bob said. "Or *you* could've."

"All right," Jupe continued. He stood and paced beside the worktable. "Let's say the small pirate hid the reels so the other guys wouldn't get them. Perhaps the pirates were losing the fight at that point. And the small guy thought your cardboard box belonged to the people in the next stall."

"It's possible," Bob admitted.

"So the pirate came back later to get the reels. But the box was gone, and the people in that stall didn't know what he was talking about. Then he remembered you, Bob. He remembered you lying near the box, and then he remembered your talking about Sax and the Hula Whoops. So he went to the business office, asked about Sax, and got Sax's business address. He and his pal were driving their van over to check out Sax's office this morning . . . ."

"When who should race past them," Pete said, "but the fastest thing on two wheels—Super Bob!"

Bob gave his friend a pained look.

Jupe continued, "They probably staked out Sax's office, saw you leave in the hearse, and followed you until they had a chance to search your backpack."

"Since the backpack was on top of my stuff in the cardboard box . . ."

"They thought you might've put the reels in it," Jupe finished. He sat and crossed his arms, satisfied. "There. That ties the events together logically."

"Jupe, I think you're really on to something," Bob said.

"Yeah," Pete said, "you could even be right!"

Jupe sniffed. "Of course I'm right."

Now the three guys looked at the two reels.

"Then these have to be pretty hot stuff," Bob mused. "What do we know about them?"

"I'd say they're studio quality," Jupe said instantly. "This is a fifteen-ips reel-to-reel machine. Ips means inches per second. Amateurs use tape recorders at half the speed—seven and a half ips. The reels you found obviously play at fifteen ips."

"What difference does the speed make?" Pete asked.

"The faster the tape travels past the recording head, and then later the reproducing head, the more faithful the music sounds to the original. And there's more clarity," Jupe explained. "That's because a higher tape speed provides more space to accommodate the highest sound frequencies. Plus this tape is wider than cassette tape—one-quarter inch versus one-eighth."

"Okay, they're industrial quality," Bob said. "But why're those jerks going to war over them?"

The three guys looked at one another.

Finally Bob said, "I'm pretty sure the group we just heard is the Barbarians."

"Which album?" Pete asked.

"Don't know," Bob said. "I didn't recognize the song."

"Let's hear the other reel," Jupe said. "The amount of music on the two of them seems about the right length for one LP."

"Hey, this is great," Pete said. "I could listen to these tapes all day long!"

"What about Kelly?" Jupe teased. "Doesn't she have anything better for you to do?"

"Oh, Kelly's shopping with her mom today," Pete said. "Fashion Island. She won't be back till late this afternoon. She said she didn't need me until then."

Jupe snickered. Bob laughed.

"Hit the play button," Pete growled. "Or else I'll bring up certain between-meal snacks or guys who sometimes get confused and end up with dates with two different girls on the same night!"

Jupe hurriedly put on the other reel.

After listening to it, the guys repeated the first reel so that Bob could hear the complete set.

"It's the Barbarians all right," Bob said. "But I don't recognize any of the songs. They're either all real old—or real new."

"I don't know them either," Pete said. "How about you, Jupe?"

Jupiter shook his head.

Bob's eyes wandered over to his dead car. "Any sign of Ty today?" Bob asked.

"Nope," Jupe said. "Sorry."

Bob sighed and looked at his bike.

"Hey, guy," Pete said, feeling bad he hadn't been able to fix Bob's VW. "Come on, I'll give you a ride home."

"Best offer I've had today," Bob said.

Pete loaded Bob's bike into the trunk of his 1967 yellow Chevy Bel Air. Then they took off for Bob's house, leaving Jupe to figure out the next step in the case.

"The Barbarians are a hot group, right?" Pete asked as they drove along the quiet street.

"Right. Their albums always hit the charts high. Their songs have mass appeal and the group is musically strong."

"Ummm." Just as cars were beyond Bob's expertise, the music business was beyond Pete's.

They turned into Bob's driveway.

"Come on in," Bob said. "We'll grab something to eat. All I've had today is a donut. And I'm starving!"

On cue, Pete's stomach rumbled. "Perfect timing!"

They sat in the Andrews' sunny kitchen at a butcher-block table and made overstuffed submarine sandwiches on long rolls. Bob got up to pour soft drinks. He had just sat down and Pete had just taken his first bite when the upstairs floorboards creaked.

"Your folks home?" Pete asked.

"At work," Bob said, and stretched his mouth wide to take a bite. "It's an old house."

"Yeah, old houses creak," Pete agreed.

A moment later Pete suddenly shouted, "Look!"

Bob turned toward the kitchen window where Pete was staring.

Outside, at the top of the window, two big feet were slowly descending on a rope. Legs and a torso followed.

Bob and Pete dashed out to the fenced backyard.

A wiry blond man landed lightly on big feet.

"You're the guy from the swap meet!" Bob exclaimed.

"Where are they?" the blond man demanded.

"What?" Pete said.

"The tapes!" the blond guy snarled. "Hand them over. Now!"

7

Disappearing Acts

JUPITER SAT AT HIS WORKTABLE AND STARED, UN-
seeing, at the two stacked reels. His intuition told
him the answer to the mysterious importance of the
big ten-inch tapes was close at hand. It just hadn't
occurred to him yet.

Again he went over the series of events from the
swap meet to the attack on Bob in the downtown alley.

The guys in the Dodge van would be extremely
difficult to trace, he decided. The address they listed at
the swap meet had been phony. And there were hundreds of blue Dodge vans in the Rocky Beach area.
With no license plate number they were shooting in
the dark. It would help to know what the guys' na-
tional background was. But "Asian" could include
everything from Vietnamese to Mongolian.

Jupe pulled on his lower lip.

Then there were the ten-inch tapes themselves. Had
he guessed right? Were they at the bottom of everything? What did he know about them? Really only
that Bob thought they were recorded by some rock
group called the Barbarians. And that Bob had never
heard these particular songs before.

Jupe smiled.

And went into the trailer. Pushing aside some fast-food containers, he sat down in front of his computer and called up DataServe, the information service he paid a small monthly fee to use.

He typed in MUSIC INDUSTRY. He waited for that to appear on the monitor. Then he typed in THE BAR-BARIANS.

Soon bright amber characters filled the black screen with information: the names and birth dates of the band members, their instruments, managers, tours, the first record album they cut eight years ago, awards . . . and the company that produced their records.

Jupe smiled. The Barbarians were with a big prestigious record company—Galactic Sound, Inc.—in Los Angeles. Jupe printed out the president's name and the company's address and telephone number.

He picked up the telephone and dialed.

◆   ◆   ◆

The blond guy's eyes narrowed. He had a cool, bold face and pale eyes that seemed to have no lashes. Dressed in a dark jumpsuit and gloves, he hunched over, ready to attack. His big feet were spread apart for balance.

"Why are you so hot for those tapes?" Pete wanted to know.

"So you *have* got them!" the guy said.

"That was a theoretical question," Bob said.

"Listen, pretty boy," the man snarled, grabbing Bob by the arm, "don't mess with me."

Pete was poised and alert, ready to attack.

"Get your paws off me," Bob said, pulling free.

Being clobbered once that day was enough for him. "Don't you have eyes? I returned those tapes to the bozos in the Dodge van."

"Don't jerk me around . . ." the blond thief began, and lunged again at Bob.

Pete jumped forward and leveled a powerful *tate-zuki* vertical-fist punch at the guy's midsection.

But the guy ducked and swerved—then broke into a run.

"Pete!" Bob yelled.

They took off after the fleeing man.

He barreled across the Andrews' backyard, grabbed the top of the redwood fence, and vaulted over.

Pete and Bob followed. They leaped over the fence and ran to the street.

The guy was getting into a red Ford Pinto.

Their long strides ate up the distance.

But the blond man started the motor. The Pinto screeched away from the curb.

Pete and Bob chased long enough to get the first three letters on the license plate—YBH. And then the car was gone, roaring around a corner.

"Boy!" Pete said. "I sure screwed that up! And with only half the license plate, we'll never trace him."

"He wasn't going to talk anyway," Bob said. He clapped his friend on the shoulder. "And he didn't get anything out of us."

Pete muttered to himself as they headed back to the house.

Suddenly the two guys looked at each other. They'd remembered the same thing at the same time.

"Upstairs!" Pete cried.

They raced back to the house and pounded up the front hall stairs. Bob slammed into his room.

And stopped.

"Oh, no." He didn't know what else to say. Pete stood behind him, and they stared at the destruction.

Posters were ripped from the walls. Bureau drawers were dumped onto the floor. Clothes, papers, pens, books, souvenirs, were everywhere. The blond guy had been thorough—and angry!

Bob picked up a piece of poster board: THE LIFE CYCLE OF THE . . . That sign had been among the things he'd taken to the swap meet. "I guess he found the cardboard box."

"But he didn't get what he was after," Pete said.

"Nope. I guess he wanted those two tapes all along, just like Jupe thought."

Again the guys looked at each other.

"Jupe!" Bob said.

"We've got to tell him to hide the tapes!"

They called from the upstairs hall phone. After four rings, the answering machine cut in. Bob listened to the recorded message.

"He's not there?" Pete said.

Bob shook his head. When the message was finished, he said, "Jupe, this is Bob. Hide those tapes! Some guy's after them." He paused. "And keep a low profile. The guy's trouble. We're coming right over."

"Where the heck is he?" Pete said as they ran downstairs. "We just left there."

"Beats me."

They hopped into Pete's Bel Air.

"What if that creep has kidnapped Jupe?" said Pete, worried. He hit the gas pedal and the car roared to life.

"Why would he do a dumb thing like that?"

"I don't know . . . he might think Jupe knows too much or something. And Jupe's not too swift in a fight, even with his judo."

They sped over to the salvage yard and screeched through the gates. Pete pulled to a fast stop in front of the workshop.

"Jupe!"

"Jupe! Where are you?"

Quickly Bob and Pete searched the workshop and trailer.

"No Jupe," Bob said. "And the tapes are gone!"

8

Rewind

"HOLD IT," BOB SAID. "IF WE GOT HERE AS FAST AS we could, the blond guy didn't have enough time to get over here and grab the tapes—and Jupe."

"Then who did?" Pete said.

"The two pirates from the stall," Bob said. "The little guy and the one with the scar!"

"This could be bad," Pete said. "Real bad."

"Come on. Let's see if anyone's around."

The two guys combed the junkyard, ignoring the browsing customers.

"Yo!"

"Anybody here?"

Tall mounds of junk stood here and there. Doll bodies, left-hand screwdrivers, car parts, mementos of World's Fairs, roller skates, birdcages—all evidence of Titus Jones's love of collecting. To him, every purchase was a treasure. Every piece of "junk" had possibilities.

And then they heard singing. They ran around a tall pile of lumber, and there she was.

"Aunt Mathilda!" the guys said in unison.

Mathilda Jones looked up and smiled. She was a large woman with a soft face, a good heart, and an uncanny ability to find chores for young boys. Now that the guys were seventeen, and Jupe had computerized the junkyard's mammoth inventory, she'd let them off the hook. Which meant bossing only Uncle Titus, hired hands Hans and Konrad, and the junkyard in general.

"Seen Jupe around?" Bob asked, trying to sound casual.

She was sorting bulbs out of a bushel of dirt. She dusted one off.

"Yes, I believe I did." She set the bulb in a basket and picked up another. "Are you tracking another shady character? Oh, the tight corners you boys used to get into! Never a dull moment."

Pete smiled, remembering too. Then he remembered they were in a tight corner right now! "Do you know where Jupe went?" he prompted her.

"Not really. He simply said he had an emergency delivery to make, and he borrowed one of the yard's trucks."

"Was he alone?" asked Bob.

"All alone." She put the bulb into the basket and looked up, smiling. "And he had that determined look in his eyes!"

Bob and Pete sighed with relief.

"Thanks a lot, Aunt Mathilda," Pete said. He and Bob returned to the workshop.

"Well, whatever he's up to," Bob said, "he's got the tapes, and he left on his own."

"Hey, fellas!" came a bright, cheery shout. "Look who's back in town!"

In the workshop entrance stood the familiar jaunty figure of Jupe's second cousin, Ty Cassey.

"Ty!" Pete said. "Hey, guy. Great to see you!"

"Boy, do we need you!" Bob said, pointing to his ancient VW.

They slapped hands and knocked fists. Ty was thin and wiry and always laid-back. He dropped his backpack on the workshop table and strolled over to the grease pit.

"Looks like we got ourselves a problem child here," he said. "The trustworthy bug bit the dust?"

"Couldn't get it started," Bob explained.

"You checked it, ace?" Ty asked Pete.

Before Pete could begin listing the problems he'd eliminated, Ty had his head under the hood and was humming to himself. Pete joined him immediately.

"The choke valve's not stuck," Pete said. "The auto choke works fine. And the throttle valve's okay, too."

"Hmmm. Betcha the carburetor's flooded," Ty said. "Hand me that wrench and screwdriver. Gotta little operation to perform here."

Bob sat on the worktable by the fence, watching while Pete reached across the grease pit for the tools Ty had airily waved at.

Pete felt like an idiot. Of course the carburetor had to be flooded! Why hadn't he thought of that!

"The carburetor's kinda like a tube," Ty explained to Bob. "It's the guy that makes sure fuel and air mix in the right proportions. When it gets flooded, that doesn't happen."

"And my car won't start," Bob said.

"Yep," Ty said.

Soon Ty and Pete had the carburetor out. Ty cleaned it carefully.

"Takin' apart the carburetor is *not* something you want to try unless you really, really know what you're doin'!" Ty instructed. "Fer instance. This baby has to be clean—clinically clean—before you poke your nose inside!"

Very carefully, almost surgically, Ty took the carburetor apart piece by piece.

At last he held up the needle valve and blew through it. "Hear it? It's whistling. That means there's a leak. And that means this little baby's the problem!"

"Wow," Bob said. "Thanks!"

"We'll have to go buy a part," Pete said.

"Don't think so," Ty said. "Check over there." He waved to the left. "There're some old car parts. I could swear I saw some for VW bugs!"

Pete trotted off.

"You're a super mechanic, Ty," Bob said.

"The best," Ty agreed. "So what've you guys been up to?"

While Pete was gone, Bob started to fill Ty in on the events of the swap meet. Suddenly he remembered the Hula Whoops. Were they keeping out of trouble? They must be okay, he reassured himself. Any problem, and he'd hear about it fast from Celeste.

"Hey. A carburetor!" Carrying it high like an Olympic torch, Pete ran back to the grease pit. "Looks right. Is it?"

Ty eyed it. "Yep. Sure is. It's for the 1200 series engine. Good goin'!"

"Ohhh, Pete!" called a melodic voice from the junkyard entrance.

The guys turned. A vintage yellow Thunderbird convertible rolled in.

"Wow!" Pete said.

"Some car!" Ty agreed.

"Look," Bob said, "it's Kelly!"

Kelly Madigan stood up in the center of the back seat, her dark hair flying around her pretty face. Two other girls sat in the front. All gave little waves to the guys.

The car rolled to a stop near the grease pit. The girls hopped out. They were wearing shorts and halter tops.

"I came to get you!" Kelly said to Pete. "This is Susi and Sandi. Girls, this is Bob, Ty, and my own personal hunk, Pete!"

"Hi, girls," Ty said. He nodded and went right back to cleaning the carburetor Pete had found.

"Do you go to Rocky Beach High?" Bob asked them.

Susi and Sandi advanced on Bob. His smile was magnetic.

"We both *will*," Susi told him.

"We start this fall," Sandi added.

"They're sisters," Kelly explained. "They just moved in next door to me."

As Susi and Sandi surrounded Bob, Kelly pulled Pete toward his car.

"We've got to get going," Kelly said.

Pete didn't resist. Who could resist anyone with such a great smile? "Where we going?"

"To the library to drop off books," Kelly said, ticking off their schedule on her slender fingers. "Then to the cleaners. And then let's go to the drive-thru for shakes." She waved at her new friends. "See you there. Bye!"

Pete and Kelly piled into the Bel Air. Susi and Sandi reluctantly hopped back into the yellow T-Bird and gave Bob little waves good-bye.

"Another time," Bob called to them. The two cars rolled out of the salvage yard.

Bob turned to Ty. "You can forget Pete for the rest of the day."

Ty looked up and grinned. "So finish telling me about these tape pirates of yours." He laid the junkyard carburetor on a clean cloth and began to take it apart.

Bob ran through the series of events, Jupe's theory of how they were connected, and Jupe's disappearance with the tapes.

As Bob talked, Ty nodded.

"Yep. Sounds to me like Jupe's okay," Ty said. "He gets his ideas and turns sneaky, but he'll pop up soon." Suddenly he snapped his fingers. "I've got it. I'll stick around for a while. Put the word out on the street. Maybe find out the name of who's pushin' those bad tapes you bought. Somebody's makin' big bucks on a scam like this."

"Thanks," Bob said. "That could help a lot."

"But don't forget," Ty warned. His eyes narrowed. "The pirating biz involves a lot of heavy competition and dough. Nothing for greenhorns to mess with." He paused and looked Bob straight in the eyes. "So go slow and watch your back."

9

Galactic Crime

"WHERE DID YOU GET THESE TAPES?" ERNESTO V. Lara demanded of Jupiter.

The president of Galactic Sound, Inc., had just switched off the mammoth tape system in his plush office. The thick-bodied, six-foot-tall man stared angrily at Jupiter and waved a foul-smelling cigar. The wall behind him displayed row after row of gold and platinum records, award scrolls, and autographed photos. All testified to the enduring success of one of the giants of the record industry.

Jupiter settled comfortably into his visitor's chair. "Let's just say the tapes came to me accidentally."

Lara slammed the two reels on the corner of his desk and sat down in his tall leather chair. He wore an expensive sports jacket and gray slacks. His tailored shirt was open at the neck to display three gold chains.

"They're master tapes to the Barbarians' new LP *California Daze*, all right," he muttered. And then he exploded. "I'm being robbed left and right! And I can't find out who's doing it!"

"Allow me, sir," Jupe said smoothly. He took out a Three Investigators business card and handed it to Lara. The card read:

THE 3 INVESTIGATORS
"WE INVESTIGATE ANYTHING"
Jupiter Jones, Founder
Pete Crenshaw, Associate   Bob Andrews, Associate

Lara looked at the card and then at Jupe. "I pay grown men thousands of dollars to trace thieves like this. If they can't figure out who's copying our master tapes, what makes you think that three teenagers can?"

"I can assure you that we will make headway on this," Jupiter replied, "for just that reason. We're inconspicuous. Adults never suspect us of doing detective work. And we have an excellent track record of solving crimes."

"Hmmm," Lara said, and puffed thoughtfully on his cigar. He looked at the card again. Jupiter forced himself not to wrinkle his nose and tried to imagine pure mountain air.

"You're obviously reluctant to bring in the police," Jupe said. "Or you would have by now."

Lara raised his eyebrows at Jupe. "Smart fellow. I don't want a police investigation unless it's an absolute must. For instance, I haven't told anyone but my security guards about the thefts. That's because the creative staff is sensitive . . . temperamental. If they saw police snooping around, their imaginations would go into fast forward. But much more of this and I'll be forced to call in the police. I'm losing *millions*."

"Your employees will hardly notice us," Jupe assured him.

"Say I hired you. Where would you start?"

"With a couple of questions. For instance, how long have you been missing tapes?"

The Galactic Sound president closed his eyes and emitted more noxious smoke. "Two years." He looked at Jupe. "I first turned in to the problem when my son brought home a tape of one of our groups. The quality was so high I thought we'd made it. But the cover looked a little different. Maybe it was a hunch, whatever. I had the tape checked. And my hunch was on the money. That tape was produced by somebody else."

"Made from what you call master tapes?"

"For that quality, it had to be."

"What *are* master tapes?" Jupe asked.

"Well, first we have twenty-four-track master reels. Usually with two-inch-wide tape. The reels are the same size as the ones you found—ten inches across. We make all the electronic adjustments on the big tapes, and then we mix them down to these." He tapped Jupe's two reels of quarter-inch-wide tape.

"So these thin reels are copies of the big tapes."

"Right. And from a set of quarter-inch masters like these we produce records and tapes that you can buy in stores. Sets of masters wear out, so we make maybe ten sets."

"Have you started making quarter-inch tapes of *California Daze* yet?" Jupe asked.

"No!" Lara snapped. "And that's what burns me up. Somebody must have copied the twenty-four-track master. Only somebody who works for Galactic Sound could get hold of it."

"So it's an inside job," Jupiter said.

Just then the intercom on Mr. Lara's phone buzzed.

"Yes," Lara said.

"Mr. John Henry Butler to see you, sir," a young man's voice announced.

"Just a second." Lara turned off the intercom. He said to Jupe, "I need to see Butler. He's a pain in the neck, but he gives us good press. I want him to write up *California Daze*."

"It's a great record," Jupiter told him.

"It's going to go platinum," Lara said, and stood. "One million copies. I guarantee it."

Ernesto Lara laid his cigar in a gold-rimmed ashtray shaped like a guitar. "I'm willing to give you guys a shot. The three of you be here nine o'clock tomorrow."

"Will do," Jupe said as he shook hands with the executive.

They walked toward the door. Lara took out one of his business cards and wrote a number on the back. "This is my home phone—it's unlisted. Call me anytime."

"Thanks," Jupe said, and pocketed the card.

"I'll tell people you're summer gofers. I'll introduce you around as friends of the family," Lara decided.

"That'll get my people to help you out. It never hurts to be on the right side of the boss." He chuckled and opened the door. "Besides, our biggest customers are teenagers like you. We might get some market research out of you. This may be the smartest thing I've done in a long time!"

They walked into the reception area. There Lara's secretary, a young man who also wore gold chains, was listening to a short, pudgy older man dressed in an expensive silk suit. The older man sported a big diamond set in a thick gold band on the ring finger of each hand. The faint smell of fine perfume surrounded him like a fog.

"I'll take none of that from you," he was saying to the secretary. His voice had a high, nasal twang. "You impertinent little . . ."

Anger filled Lara's broad face at the way Butler was speaking to his secretary.

John Henry Butler's head rotated. He spotted the president of Galactic Sound. His expression changed quickly from snobbishness to a kind of simpering charm.

"Ah, Ernesto!" Butler exclaimed. He walked forward, hand extended. "What a *treat* to *see* you again. What treasures does your fall lineup hold for me?"

Jupiter could see Lara force himself to smile and shake hands with the oily reviewer.

"Come in, John," Lara said graciously. "The Barbarians have cut a new record. It's hot—guaranteed to go platinum. Let me fill you in."

The two men walked into the office and closed the door.

"What a sleazeball." The secretary shook his head. "I wish Mr. Lara didn't have to deal with him!"

Jupiter said good-bye to the secretary and left, thinking the same thing.

◆　　◆　　◆

"Why's Jupe being so mysterious?" Bob said when he got into Pete's car that night. His own VW wasn't quite put back together yet, but Ty was onto it.

"And why this late meeting?" Pete wondered. He pulled out onto the street. The Bel Air's headlights swept across shadowy palms and parked cars.

"Are you kidding?" Bob said. "It's only nine o'clock!"
Pete said nothing.

"Kelly had plans for you," Bob suddenly realized.
Pete stared at the road.

"Hey, guy," Bob teased, "you've got it all backward. The more you hang loose, the more Kelly will come running after you—"

"Bob," Pete interrupted, "I'm not into her running after me. I'd just like to hang out with her sometimes more than with you or Jupe. And you know why?"

"Haven't got a clue."

"She's a heck of a lot cuter!"

Bob laughed. "I know just what you mean!"

They drove into the salvage yard.

"Where've you been, Jupe?" Bob asked as he hopped out of the car. "You freaked us out this afternoon—we thought that blond guy had kidnapped you.

And why wouldn't you tell us what was going on when you called?"

Jupe was waiting for them at the workshop. He looked as smug as a well-fed cat.

"It's a waste of time to tell the same story twice," Jupe said. "With you both here, I have to tell it only once. And we can discuss it."

"So tell," Pete said, "fast. My life is on hold right now."

Jupe did. He described his meeting with the president of Galactic Sound, and The Three Investigators' new job.

"Oh, rats!" Bob said. "I really want to go with you tomorrow, but Sax is out of town. I promised to hold down the office with Celeste."

Jupe sighed. "What about you, Pete?" he asked. "Can you get out of whatever Kelly's got planned?"

"Gee, I dunno," said Pete. "Kelly and I were talking about hitting one of those no-waiting wedding chapels in Las Vegas tomorrow."

Jupiter's jaw dropped.

Pete cracked up. "You bought it! Boy, you should have seen your face! Of course I'll be here, dummy. Bright and early. Wouldn't miss this even for one of Kelly's trips to the mall!"

Laughing, the three guys parted.

Pete and Bob drove out of the salvage yard and down the street.

Almost instantly Pete noticed in his rearview mirror that another car had turned on its lights and was right behind them.

That wasn't unusual. But when a third car turned on its lights and got in line, Pete began to wonder. Especially when he went around two more blocks and the two pairs of headlights stayed with him.

This was no joke.

"We've got trouble!" he said.

10

A Hard Day's Night

IN THE DARK, PETE ROUNDED ONE CORNER AFTER another. The two cars behind him sped to keep up.

"Who are they?" Pete asked. "Can you see anything?"

Bob was leaning over the back of the front seat, watching out the rear window. He'd had enough of violent strangers appearing suddenly—first the fight at the swap meet, then the attack in the alley, then the guy who tore up his room, and now this!

"Two small cars," Bob said. "I can just make them out when we go around corners."

Quickly Pete rounded another.

"A white Datsun B210 in front," Bob said, "with a Honda Civic on its tail. Can't tell the Honda's color for sure in the dark. Maybe yellow. Both look old. I can't make out the plates."

"What else is new?"

"What're we going to do?" Bob asked.

"Don't know." Pete sounded worried. He screeched around another corner. His face brightened. "Oh, boy. This could be good."

"*What?*"

"Maybe we can lose these turkeys—like in the movies. Lucky for us there's no traffic. Hang tight!"

Bob turned to look out the windshield. They were approaching a traffic circle. Four streets radiated out from it. A patch of grass with a flagpole was in the center.

"Here we go!" Pete said.

They rushed around the circle, faster and faster. Pete had built up the Bel Air's engine, so it purred like a big jungle cat. The followers tried to keep up.

"We're outrunning them!" Bob told Pete.

Soon they were half of the circle ahead. And then three quarters. And at last—right behind the two cars!

Suddenly the first driver slammed on his brakes. Instantly the second hit his brakes. Too late! The second car rammed the first one's tail. Metal screamed and crunched.

Pete quickly yanked his steering wheel to the right, grazing the rear bumper of the Honda just ahead. Sparks flew!

But the Bel Air shot past both the Honda and the Datsun. Bob started breathing normally again. He turned to watch out the rear.

The car in front—the Datsun—revved its engine and took off after the Bel Air again.

The Honda was right behind the Datsun. It started to pass.

Now what? Pete wondered.

"Holy cow!" he yelled. "Get a load of that!"

The Honda slammed into the Datsun's side. It looked deliberate. White sparks sprayed like Fourth of July fireworks.

The Honda and the Datsun sped on side by side around the circle.

And then the Datsun retaliated. It jammed into the Honda's side. Metal screeched.

"This is great!" Bob said, astounded. "A demolition derby!"

"Wow! I don't believe it!" said Pete.

"They're after each other now, instead of us!"

"Let's split before they remember us!"

They peeled off onto one of the side streets. Behind them they heard another crash.

And then four gunshots!

"Hey!" Bob said when he heard the shots. "Whoever they are, those guys are dangerous!"

"Crazy, too!" Pete added. "They start out after us and they end up zapping each other! Why'd they change their minds?"

"Maybe they brought the guns to use on *us!*" Bob said, looking grim. "We'd better call Jupe and warn him!"

"Yeah," Pete said. "They know where you and Jupe live now!"

◆   ◆   ◆

Early the next day, Bob drove his VW to work. When he had gotten home the night before, he had found it sitting in the driveway in perfect working order. His little red antique now ran like a well-oiled top. Ty had done a great job.

As Bob worked at Sax's all Friday morning, most of his brain was busy replaying the chase of the night before. He wondered whether the guys in the cars still thought he had the masters. They must, he decided. He needed to take Ty's advice—and watch his back!

Celeste answered the phone, did some word processing, listened to demo tapes, and assembled press kits. Bob worked the booking charts, matching clients to play slots.

Around eleven thirty Maxi strode in. She was dressed all in gray—flat gray shoes, tights, a long man's shirt, and a scarf wound around her shiny black hair. Gray matched her mood. Her small face was pinched and worried. Her mascara had run from crying, and she had big circles under her eyes.

"I need to talk," she sniffled to Bob. She jerked her head toward Sax's office and avoided Celeste's eyes. She didn't want Celeste to hear. Whatever it was, it was personal.

Bob followed her into the office.

Maxi whipped out a gray-checked handkerchief and blew her nose.

"He's gone," she whispered.

"Who?"

"Marsh! Who else? No one's heard from him since the gig at the swap meet!" She leaned forward, resting her forehead against Bob's chest. "Oh, Bob. You've got to find him. You've just got to!"

Bob patted her shoulder. He tried to think what to do.

After a while she stood back and smiled feebly.

"Have you called his family?" Bob said.

"His family . . . doesn't . . . talk to me," she managed to say, and dabbed her eyes.

"Oh." He sat in Sax's chair at Sax's desk. Great chair—it felt good. He flipped the Rolodex, found Marsh's number, and dialed. He let it ring twenty times. No answer.

Then he found Marsh's family's number and dialed. Finally someone picked up the receiver.

"Hello?" a voice answered suspiciously.

"Mrs. Lainson? This is Bob Andrews at Rock-Plus. May I speak to Marsh?"

"He has his own place," the woman said.

"I phoned him there, but nobody answered."

"Try his brother," she said. And hung up.

Bob got Frank Lainson's number from the phone book and dialed.

"Hello."

"Frank? This is Bob Andrews at Rock-Plus. Can I speak to Marsh?"

"Yeah. If you call Rocky Beach General Hospital."

"The hospital!" Bob said. Maxi sat bolt upright.

"He's been there since yesterday."

"What for?" Bob said.

"You'd better ask him yourself," Frank said.

Stunned, Bob thanked Frank and hung up. He stared at Maxi. She stared back.

"Let's go," he said.

"Ohhhhh!" Maxi wailed. "I knew something terrible was the matter!"

◆   ◆   ◆

As Pete drove Jupe to Galactic Sound, he filled him in on the previous night's strange encounter at the traffic circle.

"Hmmm," Jupe said. "I'm beginning to think we're in the middle of a gang war."

"Gang war?" Pete said. "None of those dudes are wearing leather or heavy metal."

"Not *street* gangs. *Pirate tape* gangs."

Pete thought about it. "Makes sense. But what do we do?"

"Just what we're doing. Investigate!"

"And cover our butts," Pete muttered. "I've got no interest in being shot full of holes!"

"Right," Jupe agreed. "We've got to be sure not to let this out to *anyone* at Galactic. Any of them could be part of the gang."

Galactic Sound was an impressive seven-story steel-and-glass building. At the top stood a huge gold record on its edge, visible for miles. A real gofer, Johnny MacTavish, met them. He gave them a tour of the publicity, personnel, marketing, sales, and distribution departments. The corridors were thick-carpeted and staff members wearing trendy clothing hustled busily along them.

"We have over three hundred employees," Johnny explained as they took a silent elevator down to the basement mailroom. Stacks of envelopes filled a table. A burlap mailbag sat open on the floor.

"Interoffice and U.S. mail come through here," Johnny explained. He had blond hair, freckles, and large hands with oversize knuckles. "Including fan letters. See?" He pointed to stacks addressed to the Big Electric Cats and to Jake Bolton, a popular guitarist with the Death Rattles. "We forward 'em."

"I always wondered where fan letters went," Pete said.

"The mailroom's your HQ, Pete," said Johnny. "You'll be a runner. And boy, I mean *runner*."

"Pete likes exercise," Jupe assured Johnny, ignoring Pete's black look. "What's next?"

"Mr. Lara wants you up with the engineers and techs, Jupiter."

As Johnny turned aside to greet a co-worker, Pete muttered to Jupe, "How come I get to run my legs off delivering mail while you're upstairs with the stars?"

Jupe whispered, "Luck of the draw."

Next they rode up to the second floor and stepped out into a foyer of wall-to-wall beveled mirrors, green palms, shiny brass hardware, and a marble floor.

"This is where we greet the artists when they come to record," Johnny explained.

"Wow," Pete said in awe.

"Very . . . glamorous!" Jupiter said, impressed.

Johnny grinned. "Know what you mean. Come on." He led them down a hall with glassed-in rooms on one side and offices on the other. Autographed publicity stills dotted the walls.

"Sound engineers and technicians work along here," Johnny explained. "We do most everything at Galactic—record, edit, and reproduce."

"Look!" Pete said. "It's the L.A. Freeways! Their sound is terrific!"

The guys stopped to watch a dynamic trio of musicians dressed all in leather gyrate and mouth words into microphones on the other side of a glass wall.

"I can't hear a thing!" Pete said, amazed.

"It's a soundproof studio," Jupe told him. Johnny nodded. They watched awhile, then Jupe said—he hoped casually—to Johnny, "I hear the Barbarians have a dynamite album coming out."

"Right you are," Johnny said. "Hank Rivers is working on it in here."

They stepped into a small room that overlooked an empty recording studio. The door closed behind them with a soft *swoosh*. Pete looked nervously at it. Dials, switches, and lighted buttons filled the room in a semicircular table and arced up in a bank about two feet high.

"This is Hank Rivers," Johnny said, introducing a smiling bald-headed man with big even white teeth. "One of our top engineers."

Hank shook hands with Jupe and Pete and gestured at the electronic console around him. "Take a gander at this. A state-of-the-art mixer, a studio's most expensive piece of equipment. Costs half a million dollars, and you can do anything with it, even forty-eight-track recording. We can put on guitars, vocals, percussion —whatever colors a record."

Next he patted four stacked reels of twenty-four-track tape that was, just as Mr. Lara had said, two inches wide and ten inches in diameter. "Our new big hit, *California Daze*. Everything comes from these four reels."

"Everything?" Jupe echoed.

"Yup. We make copies on these." He tapped a stack of white boxes just like those the pirate had slipped into Bob's cardboard box at the swap meet. Jupe and Pete exchanged knowing glances.

"Inside are quarter-inch reels for first-generation masters," Hank continued. "You need two of the big twenty-four-track reels to make one quarter-inch master. Each of the quarter-inch masters is one side of an LP like *California Daze*. Two reels can fit on one LP or one cassette tape because the masters travel at fifteen ips while the LP and cassette go much slower."

"Seven and a half ips," Jupe got in. "The slower the speed, the more sound you can squeeze on."

"That's it," Hank said with approval.

"These are already taped?" Jupe asked, nodding at the white reel boxes.

"Not yet. We keep spares around. In fact, we have a closetful of blank Ampex tapes down the hall."

"But you must keep tabs on how many masters you've made," Pete said.

"Right here," Hank said. He held up a clipboard. "We know where every master is, too."

"Have any thefts?" Jupe asked, making his round face as innocent as possible.

"Nope. And we intend to keep it that way!" Pete raised his eyebrows. Either Hank didn't know about the tapes pirated from Galactic, or he was lying.

Jupe and Pete worked through the morning. Pete delivered and picked up mail until he felt as if he'd run a marathon and then some. He'd hoped to impress Kelly with stories about their favorite rock stars and the glamour of his new job—but he didn't see one famous person as he made his rounds.

Jupe answered phones, ran errands, made coffee, and tried to keep his hands off the bagels and Danishes. His overpadded body protested at the workout he was getting. And to his annoyance, no one was at all interested in his technical know-how.

Neither Investigator had uncovered one clue by lunchtime. By then they were starving and felt a little let down. Working at Galactic wasn't any more dramatic than the other summer jobs they'd had.

Jupe had the lunchtime portion of his bread and butter "eating program" in the studio with Hank. Jupe had decided that the more bread and butter he ate, the faster the diet would work, so he happily dived into half a loaf smeared with butter.

Pete escaped from the windowless basement to have his lunch outdoors. He sat down at a picnic table next to the parking lot with Johnny and a few other guys.

Pete enjoyed listening to them talk about the celebrity artists that passed through Galactic. At least he could relay those stories to Kelly. He was about halfway through his ham sandwich when he noticed a red Ford Pinto cruising through the lot.

Suddenly it hit him. That could be the car of the blond guy who had trashed Bob's room!

Pete jumped up, not thinking how it would look to his lunchmates.

Johnny said, "What's wrong, Pete?"

Just then the driver looked out of the Pinto. It *was* the blond thief. He spotted Pete and hit the accelerator. The red car sped toward the exit, escaping!

11

Shock Therapy

PETE TOOK OFF AFTER THE RED PINTO, RUNNING AT full speed.

"Pete!" Johnny yelled. "What's happening!"

Pete didn't have time to answer. And he didn't see the Galactic tech carrying a very tall pile of reel cans about to cross his path. The stack was so high the tech couldn't see him either.

"Watch out!" Johnny shouted.

Too late. With a thud and a thunderous crash, Pete and the tech collided. The guys and cans flew into the air.

Catcalls and laughter floated merrily across the lot.

Pete lifted his head from the asphalt and groaned. Every bone ached. And his pride was bruised. So much for keeping his real job at Galactic under wraps. But even worse—the Pinto had disappeared!

"Are you hurt?" Johnny knelt beside Pete.

"Nah." Pete sighed. "Just dumb."

Johnny chuckled. "Take up circus work. You'd make a great clown."

Now Pete chuckled too. "Wonder how my girl-friend would like me in white grease paint!" Good-naturedly he scrambled to his feet. He and Johnny picked up the reel cans, reloaded the dazed tech, and pointed him toward a waiting delivery van.

The two trotted back to the picnic table to finish their lunches.

"What was that all about?" Johnny asked.

"Oh," Pete said, "some dude who owes me some money."

"Remind me to always pay you back on time," Johnny said, and they all laughed again.

Pete kicked himself mentally. By pretending to know the guy in the red Pinto, he'd lost his chance to ask the others if they knew him. Did the guy work at Galactic or not?

◆   ◆   ◆

Bob watched his rearview mirror as he drove Maxi to Rocky Beach General Hospital. Sometimes he thought he saw a battered white Datsun B210 behind him. But there had to be hundreds of white B210s in the area—maybe thousands. No reason for him to be nervous. Unless it was the same B210 . . . with armed guys inside . . . coming after him!

"Why're you looking behind us all the time?" Maxi finally asked.

"The exhaust," Bob said, thinking fast. "The exhaust pipe on this baby has been giving me trouble." He pulled into the hospital parking lot. "Here we are."

Maxi jumped out of the car and took off for the entrance. Bob walked more slowly and kept watching behind him. A white B210 drove past the parking lot. Was it the same one? No, he told himself, couldn't be. He went into the hospital.

"Thanks," Maxi was telling the receptionist when Bob arrived. She turned and spotted him. "Let's go! He's in room 6144." She headed for the elevators.

Inside, she punched the button to the sixth floor.

"Well," she said, "at least he's not in the psycho ward."

"Did you really think he would be?"

"I guess not. But the way thing's are going, he's gonna drive *me* there!"

When they walked into room 6144, Marsh was sitting up in bed, eating ice cream—vanilla ice cream with chopped peanuts and whipped cream on top.

Then he spotted them. He slid the ice cream onto his tray table and collapsed back onto his pillows. He sighed and looked at them gravely.

Maxi sniffed disdainfully. He didn't look ill to her.

Bob said, "How're you doing, Marsh?"

"Who knows? I mean, the doctors aren't saying much. So who can tell?"

Maxi turned her back, disgusted.

"Did you have an accident?" Bob asked. "Are you hurt? Are you sick?"

Marsh shook his head and stared at his hands. He had long fingers. The nails on the right hand were long. It was the hand he used for strumming and picking his guitar.

"Well, actually I've been writing a new song about an accident. The accident called Life, if you follow me."

Bob looked at Maxi. Maxi shrugged. Maxi didn't care whether she followed him or not.

Bob was beginning to get worried. If Marsh was playing some kind of game by checking himself into the hospital, he had picked a rotten time to do it. The Jimmy Cokker Rock 'n' Roll Contest was tomorrow night!

"If you're not hurt or sick," Bob persisted, "why're you here?"

Marsh hummed to himself. He beat his fingers on the white hospital sheet.

"Get off it, Marsh!" Maxi snapped. "Level with us!"

"Oh, well. You see. I was having all these symptoms, so the doctors checked me in for what they call a thorough work-up. I kept getting headaches, stomach pains, cramps in my fingers." Marsh held up his hands and gazed at them.

Maxi stared at him. She stared long and hard. And then she nodded slowly. She'd figured it out.

"She kicked you out." She turned and tapped Bob's arm. "Carmen Valencia's dumped him," she explained to Bob. "What'd she do," she said to Marsh, "buy a three-piece suit and get a real job? Ditch show biz forever? Marsh! Look at me! She doesn't have an ounce of your talent!"

Bob's mind was racing. Sax will kill me if the Whoops' lead guitarist makes a no-show tomorrow, he thought. I've got to get Marsh up and out of here. But how?

Marsh looked at Maxi and cleared his throat. "She split to Monterey with the keyboardist from the Arc Welders."

Maxi laughed. Marsh looked stricken. That's it,

Bob thought, get him to stop feeling sorry for himself.

Bob hid a smile. "Maybe you're better off with her gone."

An angry flush started up Marsh's neck.

Good, Bob thought. He's getting mad.

Bob threw an arm across Maxi's shoulder. Time for shock therapy. Get Marsh mad enough to get out of bed.

Maxi cocked her head to the side, looking at Bob.

"So, Maxi," he said, "since Marsh is out of commission, why don't you drive down to the beach with me tonight. We'll—"

"Now wait a minute!" Marsh sat upright.

"I'm tired of waiting for you to get your act together, Marsh," Maxi said.

"*You're* tired of waiting for *me!*" Marsh said.

"All these girls of yours. And most of them lousy musicians. At least you could've picked somebody good!"

Bob heard a sound in the doorway. He glanced over. Quill and Tony stood there. Quill's absence of hair and Tony's overabundance looked weird against the bare white corridor. The two musicians gazed questioningly at him. He shook his head. They stayed put, listening—and grinning.

"Hey, if I'd picked somebody good, what would *you* have done?" Marsh said.

"Split. *For sure.*"

"Exactly."

Maxi thought about it. "You didn't want me to

split?" she said in a small voice. She moved away from Bob's arm.

Marsh grimaced and rolled his eyes. He nodded.

Great, Bob thought. They'll get back together and Marsh will get his butt *out* of here.

"Earth to Maxi," Marsh said. "Like sometimes you are loony-tunes."

"Loony-tunes?" Maxi echoed, moving toward the bed.

"There's nobody like you," Marsh crooned. "I just forgot it for a while. You know, temporary insanity? Until this guy put his arm around you." He glared at Bob. "You look better with *my* arm around you." Which he proceeded to do. She cuddled into it.

"But . . . Marsh," Maxi said, worried, "I still don't want to get married."

"No prob. Maybe you'll change your mind. We'll make great music together until then!"

"Hey, hey, hey!" Tony said from the doorway.

Tony and Quill closed in on Marsh and Maxi. Tony's long pale hair flowed over his sweatshirt. Quill's shaved head glowed under the fluorescent lights.

"Are the Whoops together," Tony said, "or are we *together*!"

The Hula Whoops slapped hands.

"Unified in the face of adversity," Quill said.

"Let's go celebrate, man," Tony said.

"Bowling," Marsh said, "and hamburgers!"

"First I got to change clothes," Maxi said.

"I'm with you, babe," Marsh said, "and I'm outta here."

"The only constant in life is change," Quill announced.

Bob laughed. "Okay, guys. I gotta go. Take care after you check out, Marsh. Remember—tomorrow's the big night!" He strode to the door.

They whooped good-bye, and Bob headed to the parking lot feeling relieved. One more potential disaster headed off. Boy, would he be glad when Sax got back! This was like being a den father.

He climbed into his VW and noticed something shiny on the floor. He picked it up. It was a silver medallion with an embossed Buddha. Where the heck did that come from? It must have fallen out of somebody's pocket. Not his, or Maxi's.

Someone else's. A chill crept up his spine.

He looked around the interior of his car. Magazines, running shorts, socks, an empty pizza box, and sneakers littered the little bug. Had the car been searched? He had no way of telling.

He surveyed the parking lot. No white Datsun or yellow Honda or red Pinto or blue Dodge van. He felt like he was on the Ten Most Wanted list!

He turned on the ignition and burned rubber. The sooner he got out of there, the better!

12

Popular Mechanic

C AREFULLY BOB WATCHED THE TRAFFIC AS HE drove back to the office. Back at work, he kept looking out the office windows. When he drove home, and later when he went to Jupe's, he kept up his surveillance.

It seemed as if a thousand eyes were watching him. Invisible eyes that could see him, but that he would never be able to see. It gave him the creeps.

"This medallion was on the floor of my car," Bob told Jupe and Pete in the workshop that evening. "See the hole where a chain must've gone through it?" He handed the medallion to Jupe. "If the guy who searched my car followed me back to the office, I haven't been able to spot him."

"Doesn't mean he—or they—aren't out there," Pete observed.

"Don't I know it!"

Bob and Pete fell silent as they watched Jupe. He was examining the medallion through a jeweler's loupe.

"This is indeed a dangerous situation," Jupe mused at last. He rotated the coin-size piece. "Any sign of the chain that went with it?"

"Nope," Bob said.

"Hey, what time were you at the hospital?" Pete asked Bob.

"Right around lunch. Why?"

"Then you can cross the blond guy off your list," Pete said. "He didn't search your car. He was cruising the Galactic parking lot then!" Pete told Bob about chasing him.

Jupe smiled at Pete. "Don't forget what else happened."

Pete raised his eyebrows innocently.

Jupe grinned. "For the first time in recorded history Pete acted like an uncoordinated klutz!"

Pete turned bright red.

Bob looked disbelieving. Pete not only had muscles, he was terrific at all kinds of sports. Much better than Bob and much, much better than Jupe. It was enough to give a guy a complex.

"So what happened?" Bob asked.

"Our superathletic Investigator had a run-in with a walking stack of reel cans," Jupe said. "Result: Pete and the cans spread out to dry and a perfect getaway for the blond guy."

"It was dumb," Pete said. "I admit it. Look, I can't make like Carl Lewis all the time."

They laughed. Jupe tossed the medallion to Pete.

"There's no writing on it—modern or ancient," Jupe told them. "It's filigreed on one side and has the Buddha on the other. Since many Asians are Buddhists, I'd say it was one or more of the Asian pirates searching your VW."

"I'll buy that," Bob agreed. "I'd love to get those creeps off my back and clue them in that I *don't* have the master tapes."

Suddenly car lights swept across the junkyard. The Three Investigators jumped. The junkyard's electronic gates had swung open. How could that be? Just the Joneses had control devices.

The car rolled toward them, headlights blazing. It was a long, sleek . . . *Rolls-Royce!*

"A Silver Shadow!" Pete breathed. It was a hand-made vintage car, worth well over a hundred thousand dollars. What was it doing in the junkyard?

The guys approached with respect. The low, soft purring of its engine stopped. The door on the driver's side opened. And out jumped . . . Ty!

"Hi, guys!" he said cheerily. "Glad you're here. Someone I want you to meet!"

The three guys looked at one another, amazed. How had Ty gotten his hands on such an automotive triumph?

Ty ran around the front of the car past the signature grillwork. He opened the front passenger door. And out stepped another surprise—a gorgeous redhead in a tight glittery dress and super-high heels. The kind of gorgeous redhead that modeled in glossy magazines. And next to her was Ty: disheveled and sporting his usual beat-up jeans and grease-streaked T-shirt.

"Ty will be immortal for this," Pete murmured.

Jupe and Bob nodded.

The redhead smiled at Ty. Her lipstick gleamed in the twilight. "Are these your friends?" she asked.

"Yup. Say hello to Carla, guys," Ty said.

"Hi!" they chorused.

"This is Jupe, Pete, and Bob," Ty continued.

"Hello," Carla said. "I'm glad to meet you. Your friend just did me the *biggest* favor. There I am, all dressed up to go to a party, and my car conks out on the freeway. Wouldn't you know it?"

The Three Investigators made sympathetic noises.

"So Ty drives up," Carla continued, "and fixes my car. And if that's not enough, he abandons his so he can drive me back to Rocky Beach in case I have any more problems. I hate being a helpless female, but I'm afraid I don't know a thing about cars."

"Just a hose prob," Ty explained modestly. "It burst, so I replaced it with one of mine."

"Thanks a million," Carla said. "I know you need to talk to your friends a minute, so I'll wait for you in the car. *Ciao*, guys." She flashed her luminous smile again and slid back into the front seat.

The guys surrounded Ty and escorted him to the workshop.

"What a woman," Bob admired.

"What a car," Pete enthused.

"Lucky for both of us, huh?" Ty admitted. "See? It pays to be helpful."

"You're all heart, Ty," said Jupe.

"That's me, all right," Ty said. "Hey, Bob, I got some info for you. It's about those tape pirates we were talkin' about."

"What'd you find out?" Bob said.

"Not a lot. But maybe somethin'. First off, there's

one big guy who's got most of the tape business sewed up. But he's too protected for me to get his name. I spread the word on the street, but all I came up with was a lot of scared people. Whoever he is, he's got power . . . and muscle."

"Figures," Bob said.

"He operates out of L.A. And he just keeps gettin' bigger. He's got the nerve to put out a catalog of what he's sellin'—and there's over a thousand tapes in it! There's lots of penny-ante pirates around, but the big guy is the only one who's got top quality all the way . . . and the new hits. Sometimes he's got a new hit before the record company even releases it!"

"Then he definitely has access to master tapes," Jupe mused, "and insider information about what's expected to climb the charts."

"Yep," Ty agreed.

"What are these small-scale pirates like?" Bob asked.

"Usually sleaze operations," Ty said. "Do-it-your-selfers who make schlocky tapes and sell 'em on street corners, across from schools, at swap meets, flea markets, like that."

"Any Asians?" Bob asked.

"Mostly Thais right now," Ty said. "I heard Bangkok was the new center of Asian knock-offs."

"They import the ripoff tapes from Bangkok?" Bob asked.

"Everything's megatons cheaper there," Ty confirmed. "Costs less to make 'em there and sneak 'em into the U.S. than to buy the goods and make 'em here."

"Back in a minute," Jupe said mysteriously, and disappeared into the trailer.

"Tape pirating's been going on for years," Ty continued, unperturbed. He was used to Jupe's odd disappearances to pursue an idea. "I've got a buddy with an old Beatles tape pirated in the Sixties. It was made from masters, too. The funny thing is, the Beatles *changed* their master after the pirate swiped his—took out some horns, put in more guitar and drum rolls . . . I don't know what all. So when you listen to the tape sold in stores and compare it to the pirated one, you hear all these little differences."

"Weird," Pete said.

"That's it," Jupe announced. He hopped out of the trailer carrying an open World Almanac. "Thailand is ninety-five percent Buddhist," he read.

"Jupe, thanks for the education," Ty said, and jumped up, "but I gotta go. I've got social obligations!" He trotted toward the silver Rolls.

They watched respectfully as he drove off.

"It just doesn't compute," Jupe said.

"Huh?" Pete said.

"Ty's a great guy," Jupe said, "but I can't understand why a woman like that would go for him. I mean, look at him—he's a grease monkey!"

"It must be his animal magnetism," Pete said.

They laughed. And sat down again in the workshop.

"Putting all the pieces together, it sounds like those stallkeepers could be Thai importers," Bob said. "The guy with the scar and his sidekick."

"Sure does," Jupe agreed. "I think it's time to make a plan."

"To catch the tape pirates?" Bob asked.

"Right," Jupe said. "The master set you found, Bob, could have something to do with the pirate king who's known for his high quality. Exactly where the two pairs from the swap meet fit in, I don't know. Let's assume—until we know differently—that the Asians are Thais. On one side there's the blond guy who works with a Thai, and on the other there are the two Thais from the swap meet stall."

"Okay," Bob said. "We also know the two groups may be at war."

"I don't know why you think that," Pete said innocently. "Just because they smash into each other's cars and shoot at each other."

Jupe ignored him. "It appears they both want the same master set. But there's got to be some connection between them, too."

"Maybe the Thais are the ties," suggested Pete.

Bob socked him in the arm.

"Seriously, I mean they could have friends in common or something."

"Could be," said Jupe. "There's a big, successful community of Thais in L.A. A really hardworking group of immigrants. Maybe these pirates are all taking advantage of the respectability of the group. Using it as a cover for crooked import operations."

"Or maybe both pairs have decided to take on the big tape pirate for a piece of the action," Bob said.

Jupe's broad forehead creased in concentration.

"Here's what I think we should do. We know one—and probably both—groups of pirates want *California Daze*. They've had no luck getting the masters from us. My guess is that the most logical thing for them to do next is go back to Galactic. If they've copied tapes at Galactic once, the pirates'll figure they can do it again. Pete and I will go to Galactic tomorrow."

Pete started to massage his arches and roll his eyes.

"I'm coming too," Bob said. "I'm caught up on office work. Celeste can handle the rest. The Whoops are under control. And Sax flies in tomorrow to take them to the contest."

"Excellent," Jupe said. "We'll *all* go to work at Galactic tomorrow. They're open Saturday mornings, and the sound studios are available all weekend for anyone with a project going. They'll like having a few gofers around."

"And we'll hang out waiting for someone to snatch the *California Daze* masters!" Bob said.

"Right," Jupe agreed. "We'll stay as long as necessary tomorrow. And keep going back until we catch them in the act!"

"Except this time I want to do what we're really there for—investigating," Pete complained. "Instead of running my feet off on diddly little errands."

"Amen," Jupe said. "Let's leave early and take the walkie-talkies."

"And watch for tails," Bob said. For a moment he thought of the pirates' cars again, following him, waiting, and watching. And he felt the invisible eyes . . .

13

Bad Company

EVEN EARLY ON A SATURDAY MORNING THE FREE-way traffic was heavy. The only thing moving freely was the music of the Surging Monkey Preps playing on Pete's car radio. The Bel Air crawled toward an exit.

"Hey, look!" Pete said as they descended onto the streets of south Los Angeles. "Freedom!"

"Now we can move like a car," Bob agreed.

"Yeah," Jupe said dryly. "Maybe we can make it all the way up to thirty-five."

Jupe was sitting next to Pete in the front seat. Bob was in the back, looking out the rear window. He was feeling more confident, until he saw exactly what he didn't want to see—a white Datsun B210.

He didn't say anything. Maybe it would go away. Maybe it was an ordinary car full of regular people.

So he just watched. The Datsun was a little rusty—nothing unusual about that. There were two guys inside. But he couldn't make out their faces.

Pete pulled the Bel Air into the slow right lane. Now they were at an angle to the Datsun. Suddenly Bob saw something that made the hairs on the back of his neck stand on end. The Datsun was dented in three places on the passenger side. Bob's mind flashed back to the bizarre chase around the traffic circle. The Datsun there had taken some lumps.

"Hey, guys," Bob said, his voice rising. Almost immediately the Datsun braked and pulled into the slow lane behind them. "I think we've got company. White Datsun B210—with the side bashed in. Three cars back!"

"At last!" Pete pulled into the parking lot of Galactic Sound and zipped into a U-turn. He squealed to a halt next to the entrance. "Let 'em come and get us!"

The Three Investigators jumped out of the car. The Datsun went slowly past as if checking them out. Inside were the two Thai tape pirates from the swap meet. Their expressions were angry—and then astonished—as they stared at the guys and realized they'd been spotted.

The pirates began to argue with each other. One gestured at the three guys standing on the sidewalk. The other shook his head.

"Come on!" Pete bellowed at them from a karate stance. "Come and get us!"

The two men looked at Pete. The driver shook his head, and the Datsun shot down the street.

"They aren't coming back," Bob decided.

"They sure didn't like being spotted," Jupe said.

"My heart bleeds." Pete frowned and knotted his hands into fists. "I would've liked to flatten those turkeys."

"No, pressed turkey isn't what I'd go for right now," Jupe said. "I'll take a nice thick pizza, dripping with cheese and sausage. Plus peppers and onion and . . . "

"Get away," Pete said, laughing.

"Hey, Jupe, I don't remember pizza listed on your di—er—program," Bob said. "By the way, dropped any pounds yet?"

Jupe stopped smiling. "Well, not that a scale would register. You see, my increased level of activity is turning fat into muscle . . ."

"And if we have another day at Galactic like yesterday," Pete said, "you'll be one big muscle from head to toe!"

"Don't I know it," said Jupiter.

With that, they went into the big seven-story record company. Pete headed for the mailroom. He picked up a load of mail for the fifth floor and took off to deliver it. He watched constantly for the blond guy, the Thai pirates, and anyone else who looked suspicious.

Jupe introduced Bob around the studios on the second floor. Then he counted the number of quarter-inch masters that Hank Rivers had made so far for *California Daze*. There were fourteen—seven complete sets of masters. The guys ran errands and fetched equipment. And kept a watchful eye on Hank Rivers' studio and the *California Daze* reels.

At lunchtime Pete again went outside to the picnic tables. Bob ate in the basement by the vending machines. And Jupe again settled down with Hank in the studio. After the morning's work, there were eighteen master tapes of *California Daze* on the shelves against the wall.

Jupe took out his French bread and butter. Hank looked up. He'd just unwrapped pasta salad and chocolate mousse.

"Boy, does that look good!" Hank was eyeing Jupe's bread and butter.

Jupe looked at him, startled. "*This* looks good?" he said in wonderment. "You mean, *my* lunch?"

"Yeah," Hank continued. "All I ever get is this fancy stuff. *Pasta* salad. When I was growing up, we called it macaroni! Chocolate *mousse*. To me this is chocolate pudding! My wife's been taking creative cooking lessons. It'd hurt her feelings if I told her I'd rather have regular food. I mean, what's more regular than bread and butter?"

For a moment Jupe hesitated. He remembered his talk that morning with Bob and Pete. After all, he *had* been a lot more active the last two days. What difference would it make to trade off for just one meal? And he *was* working on a case. He deserved a little extra.

"Let's trade," Jupe suggested. "I don't mind." And tonight, he vowed, he'd go back to his eating program.

Eagerly Hank crunched into the French bread. "Ahhhh," he sighed.

Jupiter popped an enormous spoonful of pasta salad into his mouth. "Mmmm," he sighed.

They smiled conspiratorially at each other.

When they were finished, Hank said, "Come on. Let's take a walk. You get cabin fever stuck in here without windows all day. Especially on weekends."

"I'm fine," Jupe assured him. His job as an Investigator was to keep track of the eighteen reels on the shelves. He picked up his lunch papers and tossed them into a wastebasket.

"Let's go," Hank insisted. He pulled out a key. "You first. I'll lock up."

"Are the studios always kept locked?" Jupe asked.

"When they're vacant, sure. Quit stalling. Lunch hour is half over."

There was no way for Jupe to get out of this unless he told Hank why he was really at Galactic Sound. But he still didn't know if he could trust Hank. So Jupe put a smile on his face, and he and Hank left for a walk around the block.

When they returned half an hour later, Jupe immediately went to the stack of reels. It looked shorter to him, but he didn't believe it.

He counted. There were only sixteen!

"Hank!" Jupe said. "Two reels are missing!"

"What?" Hank said. "Can't be." He counted. He shook his head. "You're right—there're only sixteen." He looked at his clipboard. "No one's checked them out. What's going on here?"

"How could anyone check them out while you're gone?" Jupe said. "You've got the only key to the door."

"A lot of us have keys to the doors in this department," Hank said. "We've got to be able to move from studio to studio. Who could've taken these tapes without checking them out first?"

"Maybe somebody stole them," Jupe said.

"Naw, highly unlikely." Hank scratched his bald head. "We've never had a theft before. Someone's borrowed them, that's all. I'll ask around." He left for the next studio.

Jupe pulled out his walkie-talkie. "Bob! Pete!"

"Yeah, Jupe?" Pete said.

"What's up?" Bob said.

"Someone's just taken two reels of *California Daze!*" Jupe said. "Meet you in the parking lot. Betcha the thief tries to get the reels off the property!"

Thirty seconds later the Three Investigators rendezvoused in the parking lot.

No cars moved. There were no red Pintos, yellow Honda Civics, blue Dodge vans, or white Datsun B210s.

"Come on!" Pete said.

They raced around the side of the building to the front.

"There he is!" Bob said.

Thirty yards away, the blond man with the big feet was getting into a sleek green Corvette. He looked up and spotted the three guys. He slid behind the wheel and revved up the engine.

"Let's go!" Pete said.

The three guys tore back around the building and hopped into Pete's car. They peeled rubber out into the street.

14

File Secrets

THE CORVETTE SHOT DOWN THE STREET. THE BEL Air with Pete and the guys was hot on its tail.

"I got the license number!" Jupe said.

"Knew you would," Pete said tersely.

"Now let's get his name, address, and telephone number!" Bob said. "I wish!" Tension filled the Bel Air. Bob could almost taste how much he wanted to nab that guy—this was their first real lead!

Pete handled the Bel Air smoothly. It ripped along a litter-lined street and zoomed into an old warehouse district where Saturday meant no work and little traffic.

Ahead, the Corvette accelerated and pulled away. Pete pushed down the gas pedal, and the Bel Air leaped after it. Pete drove as if he were part of the car himself.

The Corvette whipped through empty parking lots, streets, and alleys—the Bel Air was right behind.

The Corvette rushed along a street of deserted buildings. Suddenly it turned right and disappeared.

The Bel Air turned right, too. It passed through a giant opening that had once held an oversize garage door. The Three Investigators drove into the dim, cavernous building. It was deserted and falling apart. Trash was everywhere and the Corvette was nowhere.

"Look!" Bob said, dismayed. What crummy luck!

The building branched in three directions—left, right, and straight ahead.

"Now what do we do?" Pete wondered.

"We guess," said Jupe.

"Okay," Pete said.

He turned left and rolled over broken glass until the building opened onto a dark alley. The alley led back to the street again.

Bob had a sinking feeling that the Corvette had gone straight ahead or right instead of left.

"He's shaken us," Jupe groaned.

"He must be miles away by now," Pete agreed.

"I've got an idea," Bob said. "We'll never find him now. So let's see what we can dig up in Galactic's personnel office. You've got the Corvette's license number, Jupe. There's got to be a list of employees with parking permits. Maybe the Corvette's owner is one of them."

"Excellent idea," Jupe said. "And we should also check for recently fired employees, or any who've quit. Someone who might be mad at Galactic."

"Don't forget we've got the first three letters of the Pinto's license plate, too!" Pete reminded Bob.

"And I finally got the Datsun's number on the way to Galactic this morning," Bob said, producing his scrap of paper.

They drove back to Galactic. Bob felt more hopeful again. But he also watched behind them. The Three

Investigators were still the hunted instead of the hunters!

•   •   •

Jupe, Bob, and Pete strode into the personnel department on the second floor. There was light in the front, but the offices behind were dark. Personnel had been open that morning but was now closed for the weekend.

Sitting at the front desk was a prim, pale woman with silver-gray hair pulled smoothly to the back of her head.

"Yes?" she said without looking up.

"Does the company keep a list of cars allowed to park in the lot?" Jupe asked politely.

"That's private information," she said in a no-nonsense voice. She looked up. "We don't give it out. To anyone." She looked the three teenagers up and down, then returned to her work. They were dismissed.

"But ma'am," Bob said, flashing his dynamite smile, "it's really for the good of the company . . ."

"Young man," she said, smiling a little, "how long have you been employed by Galactic?"

"Uh, one day," Bob answered.

"One *day*? And you stand here telling me—a veteran of thirty-four years—what's good for the company?" She shook her head, torn between anger and laughter.

Pete and Jupe snickered. Bob looked puzzled. He wasn't used to such quick and complete failure—especially with a female.

"Come on," Jupe said kindly, leading Bob away.

"I've got an idea." They headed across the room to a telephone.

The woman watched them a moment, then returned to the work on her desk.

"How do we get around her?" Bob asked.

"Simple." Jupe grinned at his friends. "In two minutes I'll have that woman eating out of our hands." Pete and Bob looked at each other doubtfully.

Jupiter took a business card out of his wallet, looked at the back, and dialed the phone. "It's Jupiter Jones," he announced. He explained the situation and that they wanted to see the personnel files. "Yes, thanks." Jupiter pushed the hold button.

The guys went back to the woman's desk.

She looked up, her eyes narrowed. "You're back."

"Mr. Ernesto Lara would like to speak to you on line three," Jupe said.

"Stop wasting my time," she said flatly.

Jupiter reached over and punched line three on her desk phone, then handed the receiver to her. "Mr. Lara is waiting."

The woman looked at Jupiter uncertainly, then spoke into the phone. "Ms. Hansen speaking . . . Mr. *Lara?*" She listened carefully. "You don't say . . . And you take full responsibility? . . . Very good." She hung up the receiver a little more loudly than necessary and studied the Three Investigators a moment.

"This way, please." She stood, switched on the hall lights, and walked down the row of offices.

The guys grinned and followed.

She stopped in a large file room. She turned on a

computer terminal and typed in commands. Soon a list appeared on the screen.

"Here are the cars," she said, and stood. "Both by employee surname and by license plate number. What else do you want?"

Bob sat at the terminal and began scanning the screen.

"Recent dismissals and employees who've quit or reported in sick this week," Jupe said.

She turned on another terminal and called that information up on its screen. Pete sat and went to work on it.

"Anything else?" she asked Jupe.

"Your employee files," Jupe said.

She pointed to a wall of gray filing cabinets. "Those three are current," she said. "Those five are inactive."

"Thanks," Jupe said. "I guess that's it."

She nodded coolly and returned down the hall to her desk.

"I've got to hand it to you, Jupe," Bob said as he typed away. "You've got a way with women after all!"

"Yeah, women over fifty," muttered Pete.

"Contacts, boys, contacts," Jupe said breezily. "It's all in who you know." He stood behind Pete and helped him use the terminal.

Bob punched numbers into his terminal. "Hmmm . . . nothing on the white Datsun." He punched more keys. At last he said, "I found it!"

"What?" Jupe said.

"Wait a minute." Bob scanned more data. "Okay,

this is it. The Corvette belongs to a guy named Brick Kalin."

He spelled the last name, and Jupe went to the employee file to find him.

"Hey," Pete said, staring at his screen. "Brick Kalin's been on vacation the last three days. So he was free to go to the swap meet Wednesday!"

"I've got more," Bob interrupted. "The red Pinto belongs to somebody called Porntip Thanikul. That could be a Thai name!" He got up to find the employee file.

"*Banzai!*" Pete said. "Here's an employee who's been sick since Wednesday. Thanom Thanikul. Hey, wait a minute. That's the same last name! I wonder if they're related?"

As the guys worked, excitement crackled in the air. We're finally getting somewhere, Bob thought. At last!

"Hey, take a look at this!" Jupe said. Bob and Pete moved quickly to peer at an I.D. photo stapled onto Brick Kalin's file.

"That's him!" Pete said, his dark eyes alight.

"Our mysterious blond guy!" Bob exclaimed.

"And get this," said Jupe, "he's a Galactic engineer. So he's got access to all the studios. And he would know *personally* how to make masters!"

Bob turned back to the file drawer marked T. "Here's Porntip Thanikul," he said. "It's a woman's name. She was born in Bangkok but is now a U.S. citizen. She's a market analyst. I don't recognize her. Do you?"

Pete and Jupe shook their heads.

"Now let's see about Thanom Thanikul!" Bob put down one folder and flipped through another. "Hmmm. Also born in Bangkok but has not yet become a citizen. He's a janitor here. And get this . . ."

Jupe and Pete crowded around him to stare at the tiny photo of Thanom Thanikul. It was the man who had helped Brick Kalin attack the swap meet pirates!

"Let's get both Thanikuls' addresses," Jupe said. Bob wrote down the information.

"We know Thanom Thanikul is connected to Brick Kalin," Jupe said thoughtfully. "And obviously Porntip Thanikul is too."

"I saw him driving her Pinto *twice*," Pete agreed.

"Let's check out Kalin's house," Jupe suggested.

"See if we can spot him," Pete said.

"Or the masters that were pinched this noon!" Bob added.

They put away the files and hurried past the dragon lady at the front desk. They waved cheerfully to her, and she managed a tiny wave in return. The Three Investigators ran down the corridor and out to the parking lot.

And froze.

The four tires on Pete's Bel Air had been slashed. They weren't going anywhere!

15

Space Cadets

"THOSE CREEPS!" PETE KICKED A TIRE. "I CAN'T BE-lieve it!" He kicked another. Drooping ribbons of the cut rubber shuddered to the asphalt.

"Sorry, guy," Bob said.

"Brand-new tires!" Pete bellowed, and kicked the last two. "And my insurance doesn't cover it!"

"This is more than slashed tires," Jupe said grimly. "It's a warning. Somebody used something big like a hacksaw to make sure we got the point."

"I got it," Pete said. A deep anger was building in him. He was tired of being ripped off and hassled and hunted! "And if they think they can get away with it, they're crazy! We're going to smash those crooks!"

Clenching his fists, Pete walked over to stand next to his friends—angry and frustrated.

Then Johnny MacTavish shouted from Galactic's door. "Bob! Telephone!"

Bob's mind raced. What now? He ran across the parking lot and inside.

Celeste was on the phone. "You're not going to believe this—the Whoops are stranded!"

Bob sighed. "Lay it on me."

Celeste sounded disgusted. "I let them borrow Sax's

hearse and they drove to L.A. They were just going to knock around, have some fun, you know? So they took their instruments—but no money! We're talking space cadets here. And now they're out of gas!"

"And out of time," Bob said. "It's four o'clock. They've got to be checked into the contest by seven! Wait a minute. Isn't Sax there? He'll take care of them!"

Celeste snorted. "Are you ready? Sax called. He changed his flight reservation from this morning to this afternoon so he could stay longer with his mom. So the airline computer accidentally wipes out his new reservation, and now he can't make it to L.A. before midnight!"

Bob's stomach dropped to his feet. He knew exactly what Celeste was going to say next.

"You've got to get the Whoops to the contest!"

But how could he? The three guys were stranded without a car, and the Whoops had a car and no cash. Terrific. He thought about it—hard.

"Where are they?" he asked at last. Celeste told him the address. "Good. It could be farther. I'll see what I can do." He hung up, checked the phone book, and dialed a taxi service.

In the parking lot, Pete had calmed down. He was busy telling Jupe how he could borrow spare tires from his father and Ty. Then he'd get to work on car repairs for neighbors and earn the money for new tires.

"You guys got any money?" Bob asked.

Pete moaned. "Good grief, don't ask *me!*" But he and Jupe dug into their pockets. The three guys had twenty-two dollars and thirteen cents among them.

"That'll cover it," Bob said. "We're outta here!"

As their taxi drove into the parking lot, Bob told them what Celeste had said on the phone. They piled in. By the time they approached the hearse, stranded conveniently at a gas station, The Three Investigators had a plan.

"Hey, hey, hey!" Tony shouted as the guys jumped out of the taxi. His flaxen hair was blowing in the breeze. "One embarrassing situation!" He patted his pockets as if searching for cash. And he had a few pockets—his pants were covered with them from waist to ankles.

Quill's shaved head rotated slowly. "The thirsty camel is at the oasis, but his jaws are wired shut."

"Hi, Bob!" Maxi bounded over and kissed his cheek as he finished paying off the cabdriver. "Hi, Pete!" She kissed his cheek, too. "And I don't know you!" she said to Jupe.

Jupe's face glowed neon pink. He backed off.

"Hey, this is Jupe," Bob told her, "the famous Jupiter Jones."

"Jupiter Jones!" Maxi said, delighted. "Bob's told me all about you. You're the *brain* of the outfit!" She bounced toward Jupe and puckered up.

He stared, paralyzed.

Maxi grabbed his ears, pulled him down, and planted a big kiss on his hot cheek.

"You're real cute!" she announced happily.

Everyone laughed.

Jupe held his cheek, astounded at what she'd done.

"Hey, man," Marsh said, and shook hands with the three guys. He was back to his usual self now that he was out of his hospital gown. "To the rescue and all that. Many thanks."

Pete stuck the gas nozzle into the hearse's tank while Bob told the Whoops that Sax hadn't arrived so Bob would be taking them to the contest.

"All *right!*" Tony said, and slapped Bob's hand.

"But Jupe and Pete and I have to go somewhere first," Bob told them. "We're working on a case . . ."

"That's why you kept looking out the rearview mirror when we drove to the hospital," Maxi said. "I knew something was up!"

"You got it," Bob said. He and Jupe told the Whoops about the stolen reels and their investigation at Galactic.

"Wow!" Tony said. "Galactic Sound!"

"That's big, man," Marsh agreed.

"You can't leave us behind!" Maxi protested.

"It's safer if you wait here for us," Jupe said. He was almost back to normal. Somehow Maxi made abnormal . . . well . . . almost *pleasant*.

"These pirates mean business," Pete insisted. "You should see what they did to my tires." He put the pump nozzle back on its hook. "They've got guns, too!"

"Hey, you helped *us*," Marsh said. "Now we'll help *you*."

"We can keep watch while you go inside," Maxi said reasonably. "And then you don't have to come back here to get us!"

"I say no," Pete insisted, and trotted into the station to pay the gas bill.

"Come on, Bob!" Maxi said. "Don't leave us!"

"Progress is made in a forward direction," Quill announced and smiled.

"You'll wait in the hearse?" Bob said.

The Whoops chorused yeah.

"I think they'll be okay," Bob told Jupe.

Maxi smiled at Jupe. "Please?"

"Oh," Jupe said. "All right. Get in."

They piled aboard, talking excitedly.

Pete returned and climbed into the driver's seat. He sighed when he saw the Whoops packed in the back. Musical instruments surrounded them.

"Reinforcements, huh?" he asked Jupe. "Save us if we get in trouble, huh?"

Jupe grinned. "Temper, temper."

Bob laughed. Pete grumbled. Jupe announced Brick Kalin's address. And they were off.

It was after five thirty when they reached the road where Kalin lived. It wound up through the Hollywood Hills. Tall cypresses, squat junipers, and trailing ivy lined it. There were no sidewalks.

"There's the house," Pete said as they drove past a rustic split-level home built into the hillside just below the road.

"Stop up the street," Jupe said.

They parked two hundred yards away.

Bob reminded the Whoops of their promise to stay in the hearse. "If we're not back in half an hour, call the police."

"We won't forget," Tony assured them.

"Be careful, guys!" Maxi said.

"Thanks," Bob said.

The Three Investigators checked the street: it was clear. Bob's pulse raced with excitement and fear. A guy who claimed he wasn't afraid was either a fool or a liar, Bob had figured out. Anybody would be scared in a spot like this. The thing was to keep going anyway. But Bob was excited, too. At last they were getting close—real close!

They walked cautiously down the hill toward Brick Kalin's house. A tall wooden fence surrounded it. They could hear music coming faintly from the split-level.

"*California Daze?*" Pete asked.

"Sounds like it," Bob said.

"Then this is the right place for sure," Jupe said grimly.

Quietly Pete opened a gate, and they slipped inside. Four cars were parked in the driveway. One was the Corvette, one was the red Ford Pinto, one was the battered yellow Honda Civic, and the last was a Lincoln Continental.

Hugging the house, they moved like shadows around to the grassy side yard. The windows were open above them. *California Daze* played softly.

Brick Kalin stole the masters today, all right, Bob thought. Could he be the pirate king that Ty had talked about?

Someone turned off the music.

"You've talked to Porntip?" A man's harsh voice

came out the window above the Investigators' heads.

"Yes, Brick."

The first guy was Brick Kalin! Bob smiled at their good luck. Maybe now they'd learn something!

"Porntip very sorry," the second man continued. He had a lilting foreign accent. "My sister Porntip very young. She make bad mistake."

Bob whispered, "That's Porntip's brother!"

The other Investigators nodded silently.

"My sister," he went on, "not realize what trouble she cause. Prem her boyfriend. She love Prem, do whatever he ask."

"Prem Manurasada?" Bob murmured. The scarred tape pirate at the swap meet? That would connect her—and Brick Kalin—to the swap meet pirates!

"She's got a big mouth, Thanom!" Brick said. His voice floated angrily through the window. "She almost ruined everything!"

"I sorry! Will not happen again!"

"Buddy, you can bet on it. And you can give up any of those wild ideas she's been putting in your head, too. You can't quit working for me unless you're ready to give up breathing. Got it?"

"Oh, no, Brick, sir. I *want* work for you. Yes, sir. Very much."

Inside the room the voices stopped.

"I think I heard a door close," Pete said. "Maybe they walked into another room."

Jupe rubbed his hands together. "This is great! Now we're getting somewhere!"

"Shhh!" Pete said. "Listen!" He leaned toward the back of the house.

Bob heard nothing, and then a distant rustling. A twig snapped.

Pete gestured for them to follow. Like a big cat, he silently crept forward. Bob and Jupe were right behind. They stopped at the end of the house and peered around the corner through pyracantha bushes.

There were the two tape pirates from the swap meet!

"Wow!" Pete breathed. How lucky can you get! he wondered.

The two were listening at the back windows. Their faces were intense with concentration. The features of the larger guy—Prem Manurasada—were set in a permanent scowl. The scar was etched deep on his face. The other, smaller man was the one who'd sold Bob the lousy tapes.

"Look!" Bob pointed.

Through the trees, part of the road below was visible. On it was parked an old white Datsun B210 with the trunk bashed in.

"The gang's all here," Jupe said.

Pete nodded. "Let's surprise these turkeys! Now!"

16

The Good, the Bad, and the Ugly

THE THREE INVESTIGATORS SWIFTLY WORKED OUT A plan to capture the swap meet pirates.

Pete said softly, "Let's move!"

The three guys swept around the bushes and into the backyard. They needed speed—and silence!

The two pirates turned. Their eyes widened in astonishment. This was more like it, Bob thought. They're off guard, and we're ready!

Pete delivered a short, sharp karate kick to Prem Manurasada's stomach, then immediately landed a big kick on the guy's chest in a *nidan-geri* two-level assault.

Manurasada crashed down spread-eagled and unconscious. Jupe whipped a handkerchief gag around the guy's sullen mouth and tied it.

Bob stopped the smaller pirate's lightning punch with a bent-wrist block, a *kakutō-uke*. Then he snapped a satisfying *kentsui-uchi* hammer-fist strike at the pirate's jaw.

The pirate slammed against the house and slid down, eyes closed. Jupe moved in with another gag.

Bob was elated. All those hours of karate had paid off!

"Nice job," commented a cold sarcastic voice behind them.

The guys jumped and looked. It was their turn to be surprised. Bob gulped. How dumb can you get? They'd been caught making one of the most basic mistakes—not watching their rear!

"Hands up!" Brick Kalin ordered. His cool face was triumphant.

The three guys' hands shot up. They were staring into two sawed-off Uzi semiautomatic submachine guns. Out of the corners of their eyes they glanced darkly at one another. With fire power like that, it could be curtains for them.

"We saw these two burglars—" Jupe began.

"Shut up!" Kalin snapped. "Or I'll *shut* you up!"

With Kalin was a gun-toting Thai and two white thugs. A quick glance told Jupe that both thugs were about six feet four and weighed over two hundred hard-packed pounds. The henchmen leered. They enjoyed dirty work.

"I told you, Brick!" the Thai said. He had been the guy on Kalin's side in the fight at the swap meet. His determined face was long and narrow. "See? I big help," he said eagerly. "Today I slash tires, like you want. Now I hear noise outside and tell you. Big catch!"

"Sure, Thanom," Kalin said. "Now let's talk some more about getting rid of that sister of yours!"

"No, Brick!" Thanom groaned.

Kalin gestured to the thugs. They picked up the two

unconscious swap meet pirates, threw them over their shoulders like sacks of flour, and headed toward the other side of the house.

"Move it, jerks!" Brick told Bob, Jupe, and Pete. "Now!"

With their hands high over their heads, the Investigators followed the thugs through a side door. Behind them came the lethal Uzis, aimed steadily by Kalin and Thanom.

Bob's heart pounded in his ears. These guys meant business. He glanced sideways. Pete and Jupe looked almost as grim as Bob felt!

They walked through a large, well-furnished living room and down a hall past closed doors.

"Now things better," Thanom went on. He was trying to sound cheerful, but beneath it Bob sensed panic. "We got masters. We got kids. We got guys who stole masters, too! Right, Brick?"

"You should've kept your mouth shut about *California Daze*," Brick growled. "Those small-time swap meet bozos would *never* have gotten wise to me! How do I know you won't foul things up again? You've got as big a mouth as she does, Thanom!"

The two thugs stopped, opened a door, and dumped the swap meet pirates inside a closet. The pirates moaned, which made the thugs laugh. One locked the door.

The rest of them continued along the corridor and down a half-flight of stairs.

"She tell Prem by mistake," Thanom tried. "She not even realize *what* she tell him. She not know he

steal masters from me when I take them out of Galactic! Why Prem steal? He get other tapes from big
chao por bosses in Bangkok. Many tapes!"

"Because Prem wants to be a hotshot," Kalin said.
"He wants to score with his bosses by showing them
how to make more dough by raising the quality. Then
maybe he'll become a *chao por* himself!"

"But you got new masters. *You* smart guy! Our big
boss think you swell!"

"It's not gonna work, Thanom," Kalin snarled.
"She's in trouble. And so are you!"

The group entered a wood-floored workout room.
There were no windows. Nautilus and free-weight
equipment stood along one wall.

"Tie 'em up," Kalin told the thugs.

The two heavies took nylon cord from their pockets
and headed toward the three guys.

"You!" Kalin pointed his Uzi at Pete. Kalin held it
easily, with an authority that convinced Pete he would
use it at a moment's notice. "Yeah, you. You're in
deep grief. How'd you find me?"

"*No comprendo,*" Pete said. I don't understand.

One of Brick's thugs pulled Pete's hands down behind him and wrapped cord around his wrists. The
bully had slicked-back black hair and brown eyes set
too close together. The other thug went to work on
Jupe's hands. He had an enormous nose and wild
curly brown hair.

"Don't be a wise guy," Kalin told Pete. "High
school Spanish. *How'd you find me!*"

Pete remained stubbornly silent.

Kalin gestured at the thug. From the corners of his eyes Bob saw the thug twist and pull the nylon cord. It cut cruelly into Pete's wrists.

Pete grunted.

"Stop it!" Jupe said. "*I'll* tell you. It's no big deal."

The thug looked at Kalin for orders.

Kalin shook his head. He wanted Pete to pay for bucking his authority. Sweat dripped down Pete's face as the cords cut deeper into his flesh. But he didn't flinch.

Kalin finally said to Jupe, "Spill it."

"We traced your license plate to your employee file." Jupe spoke rapidly. "That gave us your address. Loosen his ropes!"

Now Kalin nodded. The thug eased the cord. Pete's face was drenched with sweat, but his expression was impassive. He wasn't going to give them any satisfaction. On Pete's wrists Bob saw flecks of blood.

"So that's what you were doing at Galactic," Kalin said. "You figured out you had a Barbarian tape, and you took it there for a reward."

"Yeah," Jupe lied, "and jobs."

"And now you're here for blackmail!"

"Looks like it's not going to work," Jupe said. He was playing along, Bob figured, hoping to keep them alive. Soon the half-hour would be up and the Hula Whoops would call the police. Lucky for the Three Investigators the crazy Whoops had insisted on coming along!

Pete's thug shoved him to the floor, tied his ankles,

and headed for Bob. Jupe's thug finished with him and went to stand behind his boss.

"Stupid kids!" Kalin fumed. "Sticking your noses in where you don't belong! Who else knows you're here?" He glared at Jupiter.

"Quite a few people," Jupe said. "We're going to be missed!"

Kalin stared at Jupe, trying to decide whether to believe him.

The thug finished tying Bob's wrists behind him. The bonds were at that extreme degree of tightness that allowed circulation but no movement. The thug shoved Bob down to the floor and tied his ankles tightly. Now the three guys were sitting stiffly in a row, immobilized.

"You're lying," Kalin decided. "Nobody knows. You're not gonna cut anyone into your game if you don't have to. So if somebody misses you, they're not gonna know where to look!"

"Right, Brick," Thanom said. "You are excellent thinker."

Brick ignored him. "These kids know too much." He looked meaningfully at his henchmen. "You're gonna have to get rid of them."

Bob tensed. Next to him, Jupe suddenly sucked in air. This was the worst they'd ever run across in solving a case—death sentences. He hoped fervently the Whoops would get help soon.

"We must have big boss's okay first," Thanom said. "Yes, Brick? We do nothing until big boss say okay. He be here soon!"

"For once you're right," Kalin decided. "But don't con yourself that he'll save 'em. No way that man's ever gonna let somebody ruin his business. There's too much money involved." Kalin headed for the door. "And your sister hasn't got a prayer either."

"No!" Thanom groaned.

Kalin, Thanom, and the two thugs left. Someone locked the door. Thanom's pleading voice faded as they retraced their steps up the hall.

"Good going, Pete," Jupe said.

Pete looked at Jupe questioningly to see if he was kidding. He wasn't.

"As they say, no pain, no gain," Pete said.

"Ever think about becoming a spy?" Bob said. "You'd knock 'em dead. Picture the sports cars and the women . . ."

Suddenly Pete did think of a woman . . . Kelly. And whether he'd ever see her again. There was nothing he wanted more than to be driving around with her right now. Boy, would *she* be impressed when she heard this story. He perked up.

Jupe realized he'd eaten nothing since noon. Visions of bagels liberally smeared with butter danced in his head.

"Now we wait for the Whoops to bring the police," Bob said.

"Who needs cops when you've got the Whoops?" Pete said. "Four thugs and two submachine guns will be no prob for *them*!"

"Maybe Quill can talk them into a coma," Bob said.

The guys laughed. They were alive, and help was on the way!

Then Jupe said, "Looks like we've got a lot of the answers. Brick Kalin must've made his own set of *California Daze* masters. And he gave them to Thanom to smuggle out of Galactic. Thanom's a janitor, so he could take them out in the trash. It was just routine business for them."

"But then Thanom told his sister Porntip what they were up to. And she told her boyfriend Prem," said Bob. "And Prem and his sidekick decided to upgrade their own pirate business. They swiped the high-quality tapes before Brick and Thanom could deliver them to Brick's boss."

"Right," Pete said. "Prem planned to send the tapes to Bangkok and impress his own bosses!"

"So we end up with a war between two groups of pirates," Jupe concluded. "Brick and Thanom tried to recover their master tapes from Prem and his pal at the swap meet. Prem's sidekick hid the tapes in Bob's box. Then both groups tracked down Bob—and that's where we came in."

"And that's why we're lying here all tied up!" said Pete.

"Brick must be getting desperate," commented Jupe. "Instead of waiting to make a second copy for himself, he *stole* a set of master reels of *California Daze*."

"Is Thanom's sister a pirate too?" asked Pete.

"She seems to be caught in the middle," said Bob,

"between her brother and her boyfriend. She sounds pretty innocent to me."

The guys were quiet, thinking. Jupe rolled onto his side. Bob tried it too. It was more comfortable.

"Wait a minute!" Bob said. He inched across the floor to a flier that had slipped behind the Nautilus equipment. He picked it up in his teeth and inched back. He dropped it in front of the guys.

"Wow!" Pete said.

The flier announced:

**Over 1,000 Titles!
Hottest New Hits! Favorite Oldies!
All at Lowest Prices!
New Chart Topper: California Daze
by the Barbarians!**

Below, soloists and groups from many different recording companies were listed. At the bottom of the flier was a post office box address where interested people could write for catalogs.

"That has to be the big pirate king's operation!" Jupe said jubilantly.

"But Kalin's too small-scale for that," Bob said.

"He's not the big boss," Pete said. "Somebody else is. It'd be great if the police could nab *him*!"

The guys were talking about how well the investigation was turning out when they heard something familiar—Maxi's voice!

"Get your hairy knuckles off me, Godzilla!" Maxi bellowed in the hallway.

"Watch it, man!" Marsh growled. "That's my woman!"

"Hey, hey, hey!" Tony complained. "What kind of weirdness goes on here that you keep guns for pets?"

"If something can go wrong," Quill said philosophically as the door opened, "it will."

Stunned, the three guys watched the Whoops cascade into the room.

They were trapped! All of them!

17

Fool's Errand

WHILE BRICK KALIN HELD HIS UZI ON THE HULA Whoops, his gorillas went to work tying their hands and ankles. Bob watched, his stomach tight with worry. Forget the Cokker competition, now all seven of them were going to die.

"Are these the guys who steal tapes?" Maxi said.

"Quiet, Maxi," Bob warned.

"Forget it," Kalin said coldly. "It's over for them. They got restless and had to come snooping around. Too bad. She's a cute little lady."

"Hey, Tarzan, you're not so bad yourself," Maxi replied cheerfully, batting her eyelashes. "Say, where does a girl fix her make-up around here?"

Pete looked amazed. Was she crazy?

"What," Kalin said impatiently.

"Latrine. John. Potty. You know."

Kalin frowned. "I suppose it's okay. Take her, Thanom."

She smiled up at the hulking thug who was about to tie her wrists. "See you in a minute, doll."

It was the thug with the curly brown hair. He watched suspiciously as she popped up and headed for the door. Thanom opened it and followed her out.

"Hey, man!" Marsh suddenly remembered. "We've got a serious gig tonight at seven. We can't miss it!"

"No more gigs for you," Kalin said. "Ever!"

"You're outta touch, man," Tony said, shaking his mane of hair. "I've got the hottest sticks in town!"

"You've been iced," Kalin said with finality.

Bob watched Jupe, who was unnaturally quiet. Jupe's eyes were half-closed, and he seemed to be in a trance. He was thinking, Bob knew. Pete, too, was unusually quiet. The muscles in his shoulders and arms seemed to twitch. It was time for Bob to start thinking.

"Let me get this straight," Tony went on. "These guys've been stealing studio masters?"

Tony's and Quill's hands and feet were tied. Now the thug with the slicked-back hair was working on Marsh. The curly-haired guy waited for Maxi.

"Yeah," Bob said, stalling for time. "How did you rip off other studios, Kalin? We'll never get out of here alive, so you might as well level with us."

Kalin shrugged. His fingers moved restlessly over his Uzi. "We have contacts. There's always some tech who wants to make a few extra bucks."

"Then how do you know what to buy?"

"The boss," Kalin said. For the first time, his voice had respect in it. "He knows what's hot. What's *going* to be hot. But *I* heard about *California Daze* first. He would've given me a big bonus to bring it in so fast."

"Then Thanom's sister, Porntip, screwed things up for you?"

"That stupid broad! The only reason she's still above ground is she got Prem to spill about you, how he went back to the swap meet to get the tapes and then traced the tapes to you. She's some kind of missionary! Trying to make Thanom quit. She's gonna make them both dead instead!"

"You'll kill Thanom?" Jupe said.

Suddenly the room was very quiet. No one had dared use the word "kill" yet.

"Bernie and Craig will." Kalin's smile was icy.

The two giants crossed their thick arms and smiled like robots. They were killers. They liked to hurt people.

A shiver ran down Pete's back.

"I'm back!" Maxi called, and danced in.

She must be nuts, Pete thought. There's nothing cheerful about the corner we're in. The curly-haired thug tied her up while she smiled and chatted.

"You've got an hour," Kalin said. "The boss will be here by then. Say your prayers." He and his men left.

"What a grouch!" Maxi pouted. She flopped onto her side.

"Where are the cops, Marsh?" Bob demanded. "You were supposed to call them!"

"Well, um." Marsh looked embarrassed. "We got tired of waiting . . . and we didn't have any money for a pay phone . . ."

"Ever hear of 911?" muttered Bob.

". . . And we thought we'd just take a look in here!" finished Maxi. "What time's it?" She wiggled over to look at Marsh's watch. "After seven already. We've got to get movin'. We've got a gig tonight!"

"Are you for real?" Tony said.

"Hey, there's a window in the bathroom," Maxi said. "It's right up the hall. Let's split!"

"Forget it, Max," Marsh said. His handsome face was haggard.

"We're gonna be dead as doornails!" Tony said.

Quill cleared his throat. " 'And the grave is not its goal,' " he quoted.

"What's *that* supposed to mean?" Tony said.

"A *Psalm of Life*," Jupe said, "by Longfellow." They turned to look at Jupe. "Quill is saying we shouldn't give up. The goal is to live. I agree. How're you doing on those ropes, Pete?"

Pete's face was a mask of sweaty concentration. His shoulders and arms still twitched. "Not good," he muttered. "I held my hands palms up when they tied me. Then I turned my palms toward each other. That usually makes the cords loose, and I can work myself free."

"Let's see," Bob said. He inched over to check Pete's wrists. Blood covered them. "Forget it, Pete. You're massacring yourself!"

"It's not so bad," Pete said stoically.

"Give it a rest!" Bob said. "You're not getting anywhere."

Pete stopped, sighed, and rolled onto his side.

"Are anybody's ropes loose enough to get out?" Jupe asked.

A chorus of noes answered him.

"How do *your* ropes feel, Maxi?"

"Okay, why?"

"You've got the smallest hands." Jupe wriggled over until his eyes were inches from her back. "Move them." She did. "You've got some give. When you called Bernie a doll, he must've liked it."

"Can I get free?" She pulled against the ropes.

"Try to put your palms together," Pete suggested.

She twisted and pushed against the nylon cords.

"Can't you bite me free, Jupe?" she asked at last. "You know, cut the cords with your teeth?"

"Hey!" Marsh said. "If anyone bites them, *I* do!"

"Don't worry," Jupe said. "It wouldn't work. You need something really sharp to cut nylon rope."

"Like a pocketknife?" Tony asked.

"You've got one?" Jupe said, excited. "Where?"

"In my knee pocket."

The guys and Hula Whoops shouted with glee.

The door swung open. Filling the doorway was Bernie, the curly-haired behemoth, with an Uzi.

Instantly they froze. Even bubbly Maxi didn't move.

The thug lumbered in. From his immense height he glowered down at them.

"Shaddup!" he snarled, and swung his Uzi slowly, pointing it at each of them. "Got it?"

They nodded. Looking up that short, deadly barrel, they got it. He left and relocked the door.

"Knee pocket?" Jupe said quietly, and inched with Pete and Bob toward Tony.

The guys took turns working the pocketknife out of Tony's zippered pocket. Bob gave it to Tony and, watching him from behind, talked him through opening it. At last Tony snapped the blade free.

"Hooray!" Maxi squealed. "Shhhh!" she cautioned herself immediately.

They laughed—but quietly. And Bob went to work cutting Jupe's ropes. Jupe directed.

"Hey, watch it," Jupe said. "That was my arm!"

"Quit complaining," Bob said. "Pete didn't."

"Pete is physically brave," Jupe explained with dignity. "I'm mentally brave."

At last Jupe's hands were free. Quickly the others turned their backs and Jupe slashed their cords. They all untied their feet, jumped up, and moved around the room talking.

"Hold on to your ropes," Jupe told them. "We're going to need them for Bernie."

"What d'you mean?" asked Bob.

"Maxi'll get him in here," Jupe said. "There are six of us guys. We ought to be able to take on one guard. Then we exit fast—out Maxi's bathroom window!"

"Go, Rambo!" Bob said.

"Hey, man," Marsh spoke up. "Bernie's got a heavy advantage."

"Yeah," Tony agreed. "One large domesticated Uzi."

"Passive resistance changes hearts and minds," Quill announced.

"Oh, yeah," Tony told the guys. "I should clue you in. Quill's a pacifist. He won't fight."

"That's okay," Pete said, stretching. Dried blood clotted the red welts on his wrists. He kept quiet about how much they hurt. The main thing was to get out of there. He touched his toes, squatted, and came up grinning. "Come on, Bernie. Make my day!"

Pete arranged the guys. He put himself next to the door so he could be first. Bob was on the other side, far enough into the room so the door would swing past him. Maxi stood behind the door. After Bernie came in, she'd close it so Brick and the others wouldn't hear the commotion.

Marsh and Tony stood beyond Pete and Bob. They worked out, so they figured they were pretty strong. Their job was to tackle Bernie . . . if Pete and Bob didn't stop him first.

And Jupe was toward the center of the room. He was last. He would use his judo if he had to. And if that didn't work, he'd either have to outthink Bernie or run!

Quill sat on the Nautilus torso-arm machine at the back of the room and folded his arms, watching. He smiled pleasantly and nodded his shaved head.

"Let's boogie!" Marsh said.

Everybody slapped hands, then Maxi pressed her face to the door.

"Bernie!" she screamed. "Bernie! Come quick!"

The knob turned, the door banged open, and Bernie barreled in.

Instantly Maxi closed the door again and Pete slammed a *uraken-uchi* back-fist strike into the thug's chest.

Bernie ignored the blow and rushed on into the room, looking for Maxi.

Bob kicked high in a perfect *ushiro-kekomi* back thrust that slammed into the giant's jaw.

Without missing a beat, Bernie swung his Uzi, knocking Bob back into Pete. Then it was Marsh and Tony's turn. Marsh crashed into the big man's chest and Tony tackled his tree-trunk legs. Bernie shook them off like flies.

"Hey, big dude," Quill called from across the room. "You're so ugly your mama tried to give you away the day you were born!"

Bernie made a growl like a diesel engine and headed for Quill.

Jupe saw his chance. As the human meatloaf rushed by him, Jupe stuck out his foot.

Bernie tripped and fell toward Quill. With great finesse Quill pulled down the handlebars of the torso-arm machine. Bernie's jaw crashed against them and he landed like a beached whale—out cold.

"What a combo!" Tony marveled.

"Yeah," Pete said. "And Quill's biceps got toned in the bargain."

"The bigger they are," said Quill with satisfaction, "the harder they fall."

The Three Investigators moved fast. They tied and gagged Bernie, then hid the Uzi in the Nautilus equipment. Then they all headed for the door.

"Take it, Maxi," Bob said.

"Where's that bathroom?" Jupe said.

They hurried up the hall and up the half-flight of

stairs. Then they heard voices on the other side of double sliding doors.

Jupe raised his hand. There was something about one of the voices.

"Let's get out of here!" Pete whispered.

Jupe pressed his ear against the door. "It sounds like the big boss . . . ! And I know that voice!"

18

Temptation

BOB JOINED JUPE AT THE DOOR, AND THEN THE others did too. The seven stood in a line, ears pressed against the wood.

The high nasal voice was complaining bitterly.

"I know that guy, too!" Bob said. He sifted back through his memory.

"This is what comes of trusting my empire to uneducated cretins like you," the snotty voice said. "You've out*done* yourself in stupidity this time, Brick."

"John Henry Butler," Jupe and Bob whispered at the same time.

"The music critic?" Pete said. "Wow!"

"The big boss!" Jupe exulted.

"He knows everyone in the business!" Bob said. "He hears about all the upcoming hits!"

Suddenly a closet door down the hall rattled.

"The swap meet pirates!" Pete whispered. "They've come to!"

Then the closet door thundered. The pirates were battering it with their feet. Kalin would come out to investigate!

"Let's split!" Pete ordered.

They ran up the corridor toward the bathroom.

In back of them the sliding doors zipped open. Bob looked over his shoulder and saw Kalin, Craig, and Thanom rush out. They'd forgotten the Uzi—but for how long? Behind them was a large office where John Henry Butler sat next to a lamp, his arms crossed over his pudgy stomach. He looked very irritated by the interruption.

"Come on!" Pete bellowed. He reversed direction, lowered his head, and charged like a bull down the hall toward Kalin, Craig, and Thanom.

We have to attack, Bob realized grimly—or they'll grab the gun and shoot us in the back before we can get out of here. We have to attack *fast*!

"Pete and I'll take Craig!" he snapped at his friends as he passed. "You take the others!"

Bob saw comprehension dawn on Craig's face. The Neanderthal raised his fists.

Bob and Pete crashed into him. Craig didn't fall, but their combined weight and momentum made him stagger back.

Jupe grabbed Kalin by the shirt front in a judo *o-soto-gari* outside flip. He pulled the blond guy off to the right and knocked his left leg out from under him. Jupe did it so perfectly that he surprised himself.

Marsh and Tony rushed Thanom. But Thanom slipped away from them and backed into the office.

With huge Craig off balance, Pete snapped a *yoko-geri* side kick into the giant's chest. Bob immediately followed with a *mae-geri* front kick to his chin. Craig was seriously staggering now.

"My turn!" Maxi cried as she leaped up on Craig's

back and beat on him. Pete and Bob battered him
until, at last, he collapsed.

As Kalin struggled to his feet again, Bob and Pete
went for him. They pummeled him until he dropped,
unconscious too.

"Hey, man," Marsh said. "We've got a prob."

Everyone looked toward the office. Thanom stood
in front of the desk, the Uzi raised to fire. He was
twitching. A nervous finger on an Uzi trigger could
mean bloody death for those on the other end.

Except for occasional knocking on the closet door
where the swap meet pirates were imprisoned, the
house was silent. Deadly silent. The tension was thick.
If they ran, Bob thought, Thanom would kill them.
And if they attacked, ditto. Inwardly Bob groaned.
Then he noticed Jupe.

"Thanom," Jupe said calmly, "Porntip wouldn't
want you to shoot us."

"I no go to jail!" Thanom's trembling increased.

"I'll testify you saved us from Kalin." Jupe stepped
forward. "He would've shot us, but you delayed him.
Remember?"

"I remember."

"You and Porntip don't believe in killing," Jupe
went on. He stepped forward again. Bob could see
Jupe's back was rigid with fear but he made his voice
sound calm. Jupe was about four feet from Thanom
now. "Do you?"

"Killing very bad thing," Thanom said, frowning.

Again Jupe took a step. "What you did was wrong,

illegal. You sold something you didn't have a right to. That's bad, but that's not as bad as killing."

"You tell police I help you?"

"We all will," Jupe promised. He slowly reached for the Uzi. His hand was shaking. He didn't touch the weapon. Bob held his breath.

Thanom's eyes met Jupe's. Slowly he nodded and lowered the gun.

Jupe grabbed the Uzi.

And everyone sighed with deep relief.

"You are making a terrible mistake."

They all jumped. They had forgotten the perfumed music critic. He had been cringing behind the desk.

"I can make it worth your while to let me go," Butler continued as he seated himself. His little eyes darted from face to face. "You boys, I bet your automobiles are in sorry shape and you could use some pocket money to get through the summer. I have money to spare. And you musicians, what would it be worth to you to hit the top of the charts? I can pull strings and make you into stars."

There was a pause. Each person dwelled for a moment on the temptations the tape pirate was offering. Jupe thought, I could own a car at last. Pete pictured a new set of tires and endless movies and rock concerts with Kelly. Bob thought about trading up his VW and getting a new set of clothes. The Hula Whoops dreamed for a moment of hearing their songs on every radio, of no more swap-meet or shopping-mall gigs.

And then, all of a sudden, they looked at one another. They knew there was no way they could agree to Butler's offer.

"Sorry, Mr. Butler," Jupe said. "We don't do business with criminals."

The boss man's doughlike face turned red with fury. His diamond-studded fingers gripped the chair as he struggled to his feet.

Oh, no, Jupe thought, he's going to make a break for it and I'll have to use this gun.

Quill rushed over and plopped himself down—right on the critic's lap.

"What the . . . " Butler spluttered.

"Nonviolence is the mode of the future," Quill observed. "You're going *nowhere* fast."

They all laughed.

"It sure would have been sweet to top the charts," Marsh mused. "No more contests—"

"Oh, brother," Tony said. "It's nearly eight thirty! We've missed the gig!"

"I don't believe it," Maxi said, her eyes wide.

"Sax'll be furious," Bob said, feeling terrible. "I blew it."

"What goes around, comes around," Quill remarked, perched on top of the scowling critic.

They were quiet. They had triumphed and failed at the same time.

"Hey, man," Marsh announced. "We made it, though. Like we survived!"

That cheered them. They started congratulating one another again.

And Jupe picked up the phone to call the police.

◆　　◆　　◆

"So that's what happened," Bob finished. It was the next day and he was sitting beside a morose Sax in the back seat of Sax's hearse. Jupe sat in front with Pete as the tall Investigator drove them into Los Angeles.

Sax was silent. He was too discouraged to even wonder where the guys were taking him.

Jupe said, "How did your mom's surgery go?"

"Mom's fine," Sax said glumly. "Wish I could say the same for yours truly. We needed that gig. The only thing cool is John Henry Butler getting snagged. Never could figure how that dude paid for those expensive threads on a newspaper salary. You should've seen the Mercedes he drove. Big, black, and a block long."

"Sax, I'm really sorry about the contest," Bob said.

"I know, kid. It couldn't be helped."

They drove for a while without talking. Sax was staring out the window. Then he did a double take. They were turning into the nearly empty parking lot of Galactic Sound.

"Pete, you know where you're goin'?"

"To the Top Forty, I hope," Pete kidded.

"Come on, Sax," Bob said as Pete parked. "We've got an appointment. You know how hard it is to get an appointment with Ernesto Lara on Sunday?"

Sax didn't hesitate. "Wouldn't miss it for the world." He jumped out of the car.

The record company president was waiting for them in his plush office. "Congratulations, Three Investigators!" he said heartily, and shook hands all around. He turned to Sax. "I'm pleased to meet you, Mr. Sendler. I hope we can do business." He offered Sax a cigar. To Bob he said, "You have the demo tape?"

"Do business?" Sax echoed. "Demo tape?"

Bob handed the cassette to Lara. "Some of the Whoops' music," he explained to Sax.

"Oh," Sax said weakly, putting his cigar in his pocket. He sat down.

Lara popped the cassette into the system behind his desk and hit the play button. He leaned back, listening, his cigar sticking out of his mouth like a smokestack. The guys sat, too, watching Lara. Soon they were caught up in the sizzling first piece.

Lara was smiling. "Yes, yes." He nodded and tapped his fingers. The next song came on. "Excellent." And a third. "Might have a hit or two here." At last the tape was finished. Lara sighed as if he'd just finished a gourmet meal. He smiled broadly. "Superb!"

Sax jumped up. "Does this mean what I think it means?"

Lara stood and pumped Sax's hand. "Mr. Sendler, I would be delighted to discuss a recording contract. If you and your clients are interested, of course."

"Interested?" Sax pounded Bob's back, then Pete's and Jupe's. "You can say that again!"

"As for you young men," Lara said to the Investigators, "the least I can do is reimburse you for those slashed tires."

"Great!" said Pete.

"Then let's do lunch," Lara said. "My limo is waiting outside."

"Can you hold on just a minute while I call my girlfriend?" said Pete. "I have to tell her I'll be late."

Sax handed a five-dollar bill to Bob. "Here, I owe you."

"What for?"

"For those three lousy tapes. You got mad at the swap meet pirates and started this whole thing."

"Thanks," Bob said, and pocketed the money. "I can use it."

"Heavy date tonight?" Jupe teased. "One or two girls?"

"Heavy lunch today?" Bob replied. "What about your diet?"

"Eating program," Jupiter corrected him cheerfully. "Let's go. I'm starved!"